**Get into the holiday spirit with acclaimed
Christmas novels from
MARY HIGGINS CLARK
and
CAROL HIGGINS CLARK**

HE SEES YOU WHEN YOU'RE SLEEPING

"A cheerful holiday tale."

—*Richmond Times-Dispatch*

"These bestselling authors blend suspense
with a heartwarming story . . . ."

—*Atlanta Constitution*

"A new spin on *It's a Wonderful Life* . . ."

—*Los Angeles Times*

"Consume in one sitting with a tumbler of hot
mulled wine."

—*San Antonio Express-News*

D0089766

"Blends suspense and redemption."

— *The Virginian-Pilot*

"A combination of slapstick and suspense [that] turns out to also be a tale of redemption and insightful observations on how our society has changed in forty-six years."

— *Toronto Star*

DECK THE HALLS

"In their first collaboration, mother and daughter have produced a holiday confection."

— *The New York Times Book Review*

"Mary Higgins Clark and daughter Carol Higgins Clark create a winning detective duo by teaming up favorite characters from their own respective novels. . . . An entertaining . . . Christmas treat."

— *People*

"Fans will greatly enjoy the pairing of two favorite detectives—and two popular writers—in a Christmas ornament of a book."

—*Publishers Weekly*

"For fans of either of the Clarks, this book is a real treat."

—Bookreporter.com

"Some delightful Dickensian characters."

—*Providence Sunday Journal* (RI)

"The authors have created a wonderfully unique cast of characters."

—*The Pilot* (Southern Pines, NC)

BOOKS BY MARY HIGGINS CLARK AND
CAROL HIGGINS CLARK

He Sees You When You're Sleeping
Deck the Halls

BOOKS BY MARY HIGGINS CLARK

Two Little Girls in Blue
No Place Like Home
Nighttime Is My Time
The Second Time Around
Kitchen Privileges
Mount Vernon Love Story
Silent Night / All Through the Night
Daddy's Little Girl
On the Street Where You Live
Before I Say Good-bye
We'll Meet Again
All Through the Night
You Belong to Me
Pretend You Don't See Her
My Gal Sunday
Moonlight Becomes You
Silent Night
Let Me Call You Sweetheart

The Lottery Winner
Remember Me
I'll Be Seeing You
All Around the Town
Loves Music, Loves to Dance
The Anastasia Syndrome and Other Stories
While My Pretty One Sleeps
Weep No More, My Lady
Stillwatch
A Cry in the Night
The Cradle Will Fall
A Stranger Is Watching
Where Are the Children?

BOOKS BY CAROL HIGGINS CLARK

Hitched
Burned
Popped
Jinxed
Fleeced
Twanged
Iced
Snagged
Decked

MARY HIGGINS CLARK

The *CHRISTMAS THIEF*

CAROL HIGGINS CLARK

POCKET BOOKS

NEW YORK   LONDON   TORONTO   SYDNEY

POCKET BOOKS, a division of Simon & Schuster, Inc.
1230 Avenue of the Americas, New York, NY 10020

This book is a work of fiction. Names, characters, places and
incidents are products of the authors' imagination or are used
fictitiously. Any resemblance to actual events or locales or persons,
living or dead, is entirely coincidental.

Copyright © 2004 by Mary Higgins Clark and Carol Higgins Clark

Originally published in hardcover in 2004 by
Simon & Schuster, Inc.

ISBN-13: 978-0-7432-7225-4
ISBN-10:   0-7432-7225-0

This Pocket Books paperback edition November 2006

10 9 8 7 6 5 4 ?

POCKET and colophon are registered trademarks of
Simon & Schuster, Inc.

Cover art by Mark Stutzman

Manufactured in the United States of America

For information regarding special discounts for bulk purchases,
please contact Simon & Schuster Special Sales at
1-800-456-6798 or business@simonandschuster.com.

Acknowledgments

"How about writing a story about the Rocke-feller Center Christmas tree being stolen?" Michael Korda asked us.

It sounded like both a challenge and fun, and we embarked on the journey of telling the tale.

Now it is time to offer gifts to the people who supported us on the journey.

Twinkling stars to our editors, Michael Korda and Roz Lippel. You're great!

Glittering garlands to our agents, Gene Winick and Sam Pinkus, and our publicist, Lisl Cade.

Golden ornaments to Associate Director of

Copyediting Gypsy da Silva, Copyeditor Rose Ann Ferrick, and Proofreaders Jim Stoller and Barbara Raynor.

Always a cup of cheer for Sgt. Steven Marron, Ret., and Detective Richard Murphy, Ret., for their insight.

We sing joyous carols to Inga Paine, cofounder of Paine's Christmas Trees plantation, her daughter Maxine Paine-Fowler, her granddaughter Gretchen Arnold, and her sister Carlene Allen, who allowed us to invade their quiet Sunday afternoon on their porch in Stowe, Vermont, with our questions about the tree we were creating for these pages.

A partridge in a pear tree to Timothy Shinn, who explained the logistics of moving a nine-ton tree. If we got anything wrong, please forgive us. Thanks to Jack Larkin for putting us in touch with Tim.

A holiday kiss to our family and friends, especially John Conheeney, Agnes Newton, and Nadine Petry.

Candy canes and ribbons to Carla Torsilieri

D'Agostino and Byron Keith Byrd for "The Christmas Tree at Rockefeller Center," the history they wrote of the famous tree.

A very special chorus of gratitude to the folks at Rockefeller Center for the joy they have given to countless millions of people over the past seven decades with their tradition of finding and decorating the most beautiful Christmas tree in the world.

Finally to you, our readers, our loving wishes for you. May your holidays be happy and blessed and merry and bright.

In joyful memory of our dear friend
Buddy Lynch
He was the best of the best —
a truly great guy

I think that I shall never see
A poem lovely as a tree.

—JOYCE KILMER

The CHRISTMAS THIEF

I

Packy Noonan carefully placed an **x** on the calendar he had pinned to the wall of his cell in the federal prison located near Philadelphia, the City of Brotherly Love. Packy was overflowing with love for his fellow man. He had been a guest of the United States Government for twelve years, four months, and two days. But because he had served over 85 percent of his sentence and been a model prisoner, the parole board had reluctantly granted Packy his freedom as of November 12, which was only two weeks away.

Packy, whose full name was Patrick Coogan Noonan, was a world-class scam artist whose offense had been to cheat trusting investors out of nearly $100 million in the seemingly legitimate company he had founded. When the house of cards collapsed, after deducting the money he had spent on homes, cars, jewelry, bribes, and shady ladies, most of the rest, nearly $80 million, could not be accounted for.

In the years of his incarceration, Packy's story never changed. He insisted that his two missing associates had run off with the rest of the money and that, like his victims, he, too, had been the victim of his own trusting nature.

Fifty years old, narrow-faced, with a hawk-like nose, close-set eyes, thinning brown hair, and a smile that inspired trust, Packy had stoically endured his years of confinement. He knew that when the day of deliverance came, his nest egg of $80 million would sufficiently compensate him for his discomfort.

He was ready to assume a new identity once he picked up his loot; a private plane would whisk him to Brazil, and a skillful plastic surgeon

2

there had already been engaged to rearrange the sharp features that might have served as the blue-print for the working of his brain.

All the arrangements had been made by his missing associates, who were now residing in Brazil and had been living on $10 million of the missing funds. The remaining fortune Packy had managed to hide before he was ar-rested, which was why he knew he could count on the continued cooperation of his cronies.

The long-standing plan was that upon his release Packy would go to the halfway house in New York, as required by the terms of his pa-role, dutifully follow regulations for about a day, then shake off anyone following him, meet his partners in crime, and drive to Stowe, Vermont. There they were to have rented a farmhouse, a flatbed trailer, a barn to hide it in, and whatever equipment it took to cut down a very large tree.

"Why Vermont?" Giuseppe Como, better known as Jo-Jo, wanted to know. "You told us you hid the loot in New Jersey. Were you lying to us, Packy?"

"Would I lie to you?" Packy had asked, wounded. "Maybe I don't want you talking in your sleep."

Jo-Jo and Benny, forty-two-year-old fraternal twins, had been in on the scam from the beginning, but both humbly acknowledged that neither one of them had the fertile mind needed to concoct grandiose schemes. They recognized their roles as foot soldiers of Packy and willingly accepted the droppings from his table since, after all, they were lucrative droppings.

"O Christmas tree, *my* Christmas tree," Packy whispered to himself as he contemplated finding the special branch of one particular tree in Vermont and retrieving the flask of priceless diamonds that had been nestling there for over thirteen years.

2

Even though the mid-November afternoon was brisk, Alvirah and Willy Meehan decided to walk from the meeting of the Lottery Winners Support Group to their Central Park South apartment. Alvirah had started the group when she and Willy won $40 million in the lottery and had heard from a number of people who e-mailed them to warn that they, too, had won pots of money but had gone through it in no time flat. This month they had moved the meeting up a few days because they were leaving for Stowe, Vermont, to spend a long weekend at The Trapp Family Lodge with their good friend, private investigator Regan Reilly, her fiancé, Jack Reilly, head of the Major Case Squad of the NYPD, and Regan's parents, Luke and Nora. Nora was a well-known mystery writer, and Luke was a funeral director. Even though business was brisk, he said no dead body was going to keep *him* away from the vacation.

Married forty years and in their early sixties, Alvirah and Willy had been living in Flushing, Queens, on that fateful evening when the little balls started dropping, one after the other, with a magic number on each of them. They fell in the exact sequence the Meehans had been playing for years, a combination of their birthdays and anniversary. Alvirah had been sitting in the living room, soaking her feet after a hard day of cleaning for her Friday lady, Mrs. O'Keefe, who was a born slob. Willy, a self-employed plumber, had just gotten back from fixing a broken toilet in the old apartment building next to theirs. After that first moment of being absolutely stunned, Alvirah had jumped up, spilling the pail of water. Her bare feet dripping, she had danced around the room with Willy, both of them half-laughing, half-crying.

From day one she and Willy had been sensible. Their sole extravagance was to buy a three-room apartment with a terrace overlooking Central Park. Even in that they were cautious. They kept their apartment in Flushing, just in case New York State went belly up and couldn't afford to continue making the payments to them. They saved half of the money they received each year and invested it wisely.

The color of Alvirah's flaming orange-red hair, now coiffed by Antonio, the hairdresser to the stars, was changed to a golden red shade. Her friend Baroness Min von Schreiber had selected the handsome tweed pantsuit she was wearing. Min begged her never to go shopping alone, pointing out that Alvirah was natural prey for salespeople trying to unload the buyer's mistakes.

Although she had retired her mop and pail, in her newfound life Alvirah was busier than ever. Her penchant for finding trouble and solving problems had turned her into an amateur detective. To aid in catching wrongdoers she had a microphone hidden in her large sunburst lapel pin and turned it on when she sensed someone she was talking to had something to hide. In the three years of being a multimillionaire, she had solved a dozen crimes and wrote about them for *The New York Globe,* a weekly newspaper. Her adventures were enjoyed so much by the readership that she now had a biweekly column even when she didn't have a crime to report on.

Willy had closed his one-man company but was working harder than ever, devoting his plumbing skills to bettering the lives of the elderly poor on the West Side, under the direction of his eldest sibling, Sister Cordelia, a formidable Dominican nun.

Today the Lottery Winners Support Group had met in a lavish apartment in Olympic Tower that had been purchased by Herman Hicks, a recent lottery winner, who, a worried Alvirah now said to Willy, "was going through his money too fast."

They were about to cross Fifth Avenue in front of the Plaza Hotel. "The light's turning yellow," Willy said. "With this traffic I don't want us to get caught in the middle of the street. Somebody'll mow us down."

Alvirah was all set to double the pace. She hated to miss a light, but Willy was cautious. That's the difference between us, she thought indulgently. I'm a risk taker.

"I think Herman will be okay," Willy said reassuringly. "As he said, it always was his dream to live in Olympic Tower, and real estate is a good investment. He bought the furniture from the people who were moving; the price seemed fair, and except for buying a wardrobe at Paul Stuart, he hasn't been extravagant."

"Well, a seventy-year-old childless widower with twenty million dollars after taxes is going to have plenty of ladies making tuna casseroles for him," Alvirah noted with concern. "I only wish he'd realize what a wonderful person Opal is."

Opal Fogarty had been a member of the Lottery Winners Support Group since its founding. She had joined after she read about it in Alvirah's column in *The New York Globe* because, as she pointed out, "I'm the lottery winner turned big loser, and I'd like to warn new winners not to get taken in by a glib-talking crook."

Today, because there were two more new members, Opal had told her story about investing in a shipping company whose founder had shipped nothing but money from her bank to his pocket. "I won six million dollars in the lottery," she explained. "After taxes I had just about three million. A guy named Patrick Noonan persuaded me to invest in his phony company. I've always been devoted to Saint Patrick, and I thought that anyone with that name had to be honest. I didn't know then that everyone called that crook Packy. Now he's getting out of prison next week," she explained. "I just wish I could be invisible and follow him around, because I know perfectly well that he's hidden lots of money away."

Opal's blue eyes had welled with tears of frustration at the thought that Packy Noonan would manage to get his hands on the money he had stolen from her.

"Did you lose *all* the money?" Herman had asked solicitously.

It was the kindness in his voice that had set Alvirah's always matchmaking mind on red alert.

"In all they recovered about eight hundred thousand dollars, but the law firm appointed by the court to find the money for us ran up bills of nearly a million dollars, so after they paid themselves, none of us got anything back."

It wasn't unusual for Alvirah to be thinking about something and have Willy comment on it. "Opal's story really made an impression on that young couple who won six hundred thousand on the scratch-a-number," Willy said now. "But that doesn't help her. I mean, she's sixty-seven years old and still working as a waitress in a diner. Those trays are heavy for her to carry."

"She has a vacation coming up soon," Alvirah mused, "but I bet she can't afford to go anywhere. Oh, Willy, we've been so blessed." She gave a quick smile to Willy, thinking for the tenth time that day that he was such a good-looking man. With his shock of white hair, ruddy complexion, keen blue eyes, and big frame, many people commented that Willy was the image of the late Tip O'Neill, the legendary Speaker of the House of Representatives.

The light turned green. They crossed Fifth Avenue and walked along Central Park South to their apartment just past Seventh Avenue. Alvirah pointed to a young couple who were getting into a horse-drawn carriage for a ride through the park. "I wonder if he's going to propose to her," she commented. "Remember that's where you proposed to me?"

"Sure I remember," Willy said, "and the whole time I was hoping I had enough money to pay for the ride. In the restaurant I meant to tip the headwaiter five bucks, and like a dope I gave him fifty. Didn't realize it until I reached for the ring to put on your finger. Anyhow, I'm glad we decided to go to Vermont with the Reillys. Maybe we'll take a ride on one of the horse-drawn sleighs up there."

"Well, for sure I won't go downhill skiing," Alvirah said. "That's why I hesitated when Regan suggested we go. She and Jack and Nora and Luke are all great skiers. But we can go cross-country skiing, I've got books I want to read, and there are walking paths. One way or another we'll find plenty to do."

Fifteen minutes later, in their comfortable living room with its sweeping view of Central Park, she was opening the package the doorman had given her. "Willy, I don't believe it," she said. "Not even Thanksgiving, yet, and Molloy, McDermott, McFadden, and Markey are sending us a Christmas present." The Four M's, as the brokerage firm was known on Wall Street, was the one Alvirah and Willy had selected to handle the money they allocated to buying government bonds or stock in rock-solid companies.

"What'd they send us?" Willy called from the kitchen as he prepared manhattans, their favorite five o'clock cocktail.

"I haven't opened it yet," Alvirah called back. "You know all that plastic they put on everything. But I think it's a bottle or a jar. The card says 'Happy Holidays.' Boy are they rushing the season. It's not even Thanksgiving yet."

"Whatever it is, don't ruin your nails," Willy warned. "I'll get it for you."

Don't ruin your nails. Alvirah smiled to herself remembering the years when it would have been a waste of time to put even a dab of polish on her nails because all the bleaches and harsh soaps she used cleaning houses would have made short work of it.

Willy came into the living room carrying a tray with two cocktail glasses and a plate of cheese and crackers. Herman's idea of nourishment at the meeting had been Twinkies and instant coffee, both of which Willy and Alvirah had refused.

He put the tray on the coffee table and picked up the bubble-wrapped package. With a firm thrust he pulled apart the adhesive seals and unwound the wrapping. His expression of anticipation changed to surprise and then amazement.

14

"How much money have we got invested with the Four M's?" he asked.

Alvirah told him.

"Honey, take a look. They sent us a jar of maple syrup. That's their idea of a Christmas present?"

"They've got to be kidding," Alvirah exclaimed, shaking her head as she took the jar from him. Then she read the label. "Willy, look," she exclaimed. "They didn't give us just a jar of syrup. They gave us a *tree!* It says so right here. *'This syrup comes from the tree reserved for Willy and Alvirah Meehan. Please come and tap your tree to refill this jar when it is empty.'* I wonder where the tree is."

Willy began rummaging through the gift-wrapped box that had contained the jar. "Here's a paper. No, it's a map." He studied it and began to laugh. "Honey, here's something else we can do when we're in Stowe. We can look up our tree. From the way it looks here, it's right near the Trapp family property."

The phone rang. It was Regan Reilly calling

15

from Los Angeles. "All set for Vermont?" she asked. "No backing out now, promise?"

"Not a chance, Regan," Alvirah assured her. "I've got business in Stowe. I'm going to look up a tree."

3

egan, you must be exhausted," Nora Regan Reilly said with concern, as she looked fondly across the breakfast table at her only child. To others, beautiful raven-haired Regan might be a superb private investigator, but to Nora, her thirty-one-year-old daughter was still the little girl she would give her life to protect.

"She looks okay to me," Luke Reilly observed as he set down his coffee cup with the decisive gesture that said he was on his way. His lanky six-foot-five frame was encased in a midnight blue suit, white shirt, and black tie, one of the half-dozen such outfits in his possession. Luke was the owner of three funeral homes in northern New Jersey, which was the reason for his need for subdued clothing. His handsome head of silver hair complemented his lean face, which could look suitably somber but always broke into a ready smile outside his viewing rooms. Now that smile encompassed both his wife and his daughter.

They were at the breakfast table in the Reilly home in Summit, New Jersey, the home in which Regan had grown up and where Luke and Nora still lived. It was also the place where Nora Regan Reilly wrote the suspense novels that had made her famous. Now she got up to kiss her husband good-bye. Ever since he'd been kidnapped a year ago, he never walked out the door without her worrying that something might happen to him.

Like Regan, Nora had classic features, blue eyes, and fair skin. Unlike Regan, she was a natural blond. At five feet three, she was four inches shorter than her daughter and towered over by her husband.

"Don't get kidnapped," she said only half-jokingly. "We want to leave for Vermont no later than two o'clock."

"Getting kidnapped once in a lifetime is about average," Regan volunteered. "I looked up the statistics last week."

"And don't forget," Luke reminded Nora for the hundredth time, "if it wasn't for my pain and suffering in that little predicament, Regan would never have met Jack and you wouldn't be planning a wedding."

Jack Reilly, head of the Major Case Squad of the New York Police Department and now Regan's fiancé, had worked on the case when Luke and his young driver vanished. He not only caught the kidnappers and retrieved the ransom, but in the process had captured Regan's heart.

"I can't believe I haven't seen Jack in two weeks," Regan said with a sigh as she buttered a roll. "He wanted to pick me up at Newark Airport this morning, but I told him I'd take a cab. He had to go into the office to wrap up a few things but he'll be here by two." Regan started to yawn. "Those overnight flights make me a little spacey."

"On second thought, I would suggest that your mother is right," Luke said. "You do look as if a couple of hours of sleep would be useful." He returned Nora's kiss, rumpled Regan's hair, and was gone.

Regan laughed. "I swear he still thinks I'm six years old."

"It's because you're getting married soon. He's starting to talk about how he's looking forward to grandchildren."

"Oh, my God. That thought makes me even more tired. I think I will go upstairs and lie down."

Left alone at the table, Nora refilled her own cup and opened *The New York Times*. The car was already packed for the trip. This morning she intended to work at her desk because she wanted to make notes on the new book she was starting. She hadn't quite decided whether Celia, her protagonist, would be an interior designer or a lawyer. Two different kinds of people, she acknowledged, but as an interior designer it was feasible that Celia would have met her first husband in the process of decorating his Manhattan apartment. On the other hand, if she was a lawyer, it gave a different dynamic to the story.

Read the paper, she told herself. First lesson of writing: Put the subconscious on power-save until you start staring at the computer. She glanced out the window. The breakfast room looked out onto the now snow-covered lawn and the garden that led to the pool and tennis court. I love it here, she thought. I get so mad at the people who knock New Jersey. Oh, well, as Dad used to say, "When they know better, they'll do better."

Wrapped in her quilted satin bathrobe, Nora felt warm and content. Instead of chasing crooks in Los Angeles, Regan was home and going away with them. She had gotten engaged in a hot air balloon, of all places, just a few weeks ago. Over Las Vegas. Nora didn't care where or how it happened, she was just thrilled to finally be planning Regan's wedding. And there couldn't be a more perfect man for her than wonderful Jack Reilly.

In a few hours they would be leaving for the

beautiful Trapp Family Lodge and would be joined there by their dear friends Alvirah and Willy Meehan. What's not to like? Nora thought as she flipped to the Metro section of the newspaper.

Her eye immediately went to the front-page picture of a handsome woman dressed in a long skirt, blouse, and vest and standing in a forest. The caption was "Rockefeller Center Selects Tree."

The woman in that picture looks familiar, Nora thought as she skimmed the story.

An 80-foot blue spruce in Stowe, Vermont, is about to take its place as the world's most famous Christmas tree this year. It was chosen for its majestic beauty, but as it turned out, it was planted nearly fifty years ago in a forest adjacent to the property owned by the legendary Von Trapp family. Maria von Trapp happened to be walking through the forest when the sapling was planted, and her picture was taken standing next to it. Since the fortieth anniversary of the world's most successful musical film, *The Sound of Music,* is about to occur, and since the film emphasizes family values and courage in the face of adversity, a special reception has been planned for the tree on its arrival in New York.

It will be cut down on Monday morning and then taken on a flatbed to a barge near New Haven and floated down Long Island Sound to Manhattan. Upon its arrival at Rockefeller Center it will be greeted by a choir of hundreds of schoolchildren from all over the city who will sing a medley of songs from *The Sound of Music.*

"Well, for heaven's sake," Nora said aloud. "They'll be cutting down the tree while we're there. What fun it will be to watch." She began to hum: " 'The hills are alive . . .' "

4

On that same morning a scant hundred miles away, Packy Noonan woke up with a happy smile plastered on his face.

"It's your big day, huh, Packy?" C.R., the racketeer in the next cell, asked sourly.

Packy could understand the reason for his sullen manner. C.R. was in only the second year of a fourteen-year stretch, and he had not yet adjusted to life behind bars.

"It's my big day," Packy agreed amiably as he packed his few possessions: toiletries, underwear, socks, and a picture of his long-dead mother. He always referred to her lovingly and with tears in his eyes when he spoke in the chapel in his role as a counselor to his fellow inmates. He explained to them that she had always seen the good in him even when he had gone astray, and on her deathbed she told him that she knew he'd turn out to be an upstanding citizen.

In fact, he hadn't seen his mother for twenty years before she died. Nor did he see fit to share with his fellow inmates the fact that in her will, after leaving her meager possessions to the Sisters of Charity, she had written, "And to my son, Patrick, unfortunately known as Packy, I leave one dollar and his high chair because the only time he ever gave me any happiness was when he was small enough to sit in it."

Ma had a way with words, Packy thought fondly. I guess I got the gift of gab from her. The woman on the parole board had almost been in tears when he had explained at his hearing that he prayed to his mother every night. Not that it had done him any good. He had served every last day of his minimum sentence plus another two years. The bleeding heart had been overruled by the rest of the board, six to one.

The jacket and slacks he had worn when he arrived at the prison were out of fashion, of course, but it felt great to put them on. And thanks to the money he swindled, they had been custom-made by Armani. As far as he was concerned, he still looked pretty sharp in them—not that they would be in his closet for thirty seconds after he got to Brazil.

His lawyer, Thoris Twinning, was picking him up at ten o'clock to escort him to the halfway house known as The Castle on the Upper West Side in Manhattan. Packy loved the story that in its long history The Castle had twice been an academy for Catholic high school girls. Ma should know that, he thought. She'd think I was defiling the place.

He was scheduled to stay there for two weeks to reintroduce himself to the world where people actually worked for a living. He understood that there would be group sessions in which the rules about signing in and signing out and the importance of reporting to his parole officer would be explained. He was assured that at The Castle they would be able to find him permanent housing. He could predict that it would be in a crummy rooming house in Staten Island or the Bronx. The counselors would also help him get a job immediately.

Packy could hardly wait. He knew that the receiver appointed by the Bureau of Securities to try to find the money lost by the investors would probably have him tailed. There was nothing he looked forward to more than the fun of losing that tail. Unlike thirteen years ago when detectives were swarming all over Manhattan looking for him. He was just leaving for Vermont to retrieve the loot and get out of the country when he was arrested. That wasn't going to happen again.

It had already been explained to him that as of Sunday he would be allowed to leave The Castle in the morning but had to be back and signed in by dinner time. And he had already figured out exactly how he would shake the nincompoop who was supposed to be following him.

At ten-forty on Sunday morning, Benny and Jo-Jo would be waiting on Madison and Fifty-first in a van with a ski rack. Then they'd be on their way to Vermont. Following his instructions, Benny and Jo-Jo had rented a farm near Stowe six months ago. The only virtue of the farm was that it had a large if decrepit barn where a flatbed would be housed.

In the farmhouse the twins had installed an acquaintance, a guy without a record who was incredibly naive and was happy to be paid to house sit for them.

That way, just in case there were any slips, when the cops were searching for a flatbed with a tree on it, they wouldn't start looking in places where people lived. There were enough farms with barns that were owned by out-of-town skiers for them to investigate. The skiers usually didn't arrive until after Thanksgiving.

I wired the flask of diamonds onto the branch thirteen and a half years ago, Packy thought. A spruce grows about one and a half feet a year. The branch I marked was about twenty feet high at the time. I was standing at the top of the twenty foot ladder. Now that branch should be about forty feet high. Trouble is no regular ladder goes that high.

That's why we have to take the whole tree, and if someone with nothing better to do than mind other people's business asks questions, we can say it's going to be decorated for the Christmas pageant in Hackensack, New Jersey. Jo-Jo has a fake permit to cut the tree and a phony letter from the mayor of Hackensack, thanking Pickens for the tree, so that should take care of that.

Packy's agile brain leaped about to find any flaw in his reasoning but came up dry. Satisfied, he continued to review the plan: Then we get the flatbed into the barn, find the branch where the loot is hidden, and then we're off to Brazil, cha, cha, cha.

All of the above was racing through Packy's mind as he ate his final breakfast at the Federal Correctional Institution and, when it was over, bid a fond farewell to his fellow inmates.

"Good luck, Packy," Lightfingered Tom said solemnly.

"Don't give up preaching," a grizzled long-timer urged. "Keep that promise to your mother that you'd set a good example for the young."

Ed, the lawyer who had vacated his clients' trust funds of millions, grinned and gave a lazy wave of his hand. "I give you three months before you're back," he predicted.

Packy didn't show how much that got under his skin. "I'll send you a card, Ed," he said. "From Brazil," he muttered under his breath as he followed the guard to the warden's office where Thoris Twinning, his court-appointed lawyer, was waiting.

Thoris was beaming. "A happy day," he gushed. "A happy, happy day. And I have wonderful news. I've been in touch with your parole officer, and he has a job for you. As of a week from Monday you will be working at the salad bar in the Palace-Plus diner on Broadway and Ninety-seventh Street."

As of a week from Monday a bunch of lackeys will be dropping grapes into my mouth, Packy thought, but he turned on the mesmerizing smile that had enchanted Opal Fogarty and some two hundred other investors in the Patrick Noonan Shipping and Handling Company. "My mama's prayers have been answered," he said joyfully. His eyes raised to heaven and a blissful expression on his sharp-featured face, he sighed, "An honest job with an honest day's pay. Just what Mama always wanted for me."

5

y, my, this is such a beautiful car," Opal Fogarty commented from the back seat of Alvirah and Willy's Mercedes. "When I was growing up we had a pickup truck. My father said it made him feel like a cowboy. My mother used to tell him it rode like a bucking steer, so she could understand why he felt like a cowboy. He bought it without telling her, and boy was she mad! But I have to say this: It lasted for fourteen years before it stopped dead on the Triborough Bridge during rush hour. Even my father admitted it was time to give up on the truck, and this time my mother went car shopping with him." She laughed. "She got to pick out the car. It was a Dodge. Daddy made her mad by asking the salesman if a taxi meter was an option."

Alvirah turned to look at Opal. "Why did he ask that?"

"Honey, it's because Dodge made so many taxis," Willy explained. "That was funny, Opal."

"Dad *was* pretty funny," Opal agreed. "He never had two nickels to rub together, but he did his best. He inherited two thousand dollars when I was about eight years old, and somebody convinced him to put it in parachute stock. They said that with all the commercial flying people would be doing, all the passengers would have to wear parachutes. I guess being gullible is genetic."

Alvirah was glad to hear Opal laugh. It was two o'clock, and they were on route 91 heading for Vermont. At ten o'clock she and Willy had been packing for the trip and half-watching the television in the bedroom when a news flash caught their attention. It showed Packy Noonan leaving federal prison in his lawyer's car. At the gate he got out of the car and spoke to the reporters. "I regret the harm I have caused the investors in my company," he said. Tears welled in his eyes and his lip trembled as he went on. "I understand that I will be working at the salad bar at the Palace-Plus diner, and I will ask that ten percent of my wages be taken to start to repay the people who lost their savings in the Patrick Noonan Shipping and Handling Company."

"Ten percent of a minimum wage job!" Willy had snorted. "He's got to be kidding."

Alvirah had rushed to the phone and dialed Opal. "Turn on channel twenty-four!" she ordered. Then she was sorry she had made the call because when Opal saw Packy, she began to cry.

"Oh, Alvirah, it just makes me sick to think that terrible cheat is as free as a daisy while I'm sitting here thrilled to get a week's vacation because I'm so tired. Mark my words, he'll end up joining his pals on the Riviera or wherever they are with my money in their pockets."

That was when Alvirah insisted that Opal

join them for the long weekend in Vermont. "We have two big bedrooms and baths in our villa," she said, "and it will do you good to get away. You can help us follow the map and find my tree. There won't be any syrup coming from it now, but I packed the jar that the stockbrokers sent me. We have a little kitchen so maybe I'll make pancakes for everyone and see how good the syrup tastes. And I read in the paper that they'll be cutting down the tree for Rockefeller Center right near where we're staying. That would be fun to watch, wouldn't it?"

It didn't take much to persuade Opal. And she was already perking up. On the trip to Vermont she made only one comment about Packy Noonan: "I can just see him working at a salad bar in a diner. He'll probably be sneaking the croutons into his pocket."

6

Sometimes Milo Brosky wished he had
never met the Como twins. He had run into
them by chance in Greenwich Village twenty
years ago when he attended a poets' meeting in
the back room of Eddie's Aurora. Benny and
Jo-Jo were hanging out in the bar.

I was feeling pretty good, Milo thought as he
sipped a beer in the shabby parlor of a rundown
farmhouse in Stowe, Vermont. I'd just read my
narrative poem about a peach who falls in love
with a fruit fly, and our workshop thought it was
wonderful. They saw deep meaning and ten-
derness that never verged on sentimentality in

my poem. I felt so good I decided to have a beer on the way home, and that's when I met the twins.

Milo took another sip of beer. I should have bought back my introduction to them, he thought glumly. Not that they weren't good to me. They knew that I hadn't had my big break-through as a poet and that I'd take any kind of job to keep a roof over my head. But this roof feels as though it could fall in on me. They're up to something.

Milo frowned. Forty-two years old, with shoulder-length hair and a wispy beard, he could have been an extra in a film about Woodstock '69. His bony arms dangled from his long frame. His guileless gray eyes had a perpetually benevolent expression. His voice with its singsong pitch made his listeners think of adjectives like "kind" and "gentle."

Milo knew that a dozen years ago the Como Brothers had been obliged to skip town in a hurry because of their involvement with the Packy Noonan scam. He hadn't heard from them in years. Then six months ago he had re-

ceived a phone call from Jo-Jo. He wouldn't
say where he was, but he asked Milo if he
would be interested in making a lot of money
without any risk. All Milo had to do was find a
farmhouse for rent in Stowe, Vermont. It had
to have a large barn, at least ninety feet long.
Until the first of the year Milo was to spend at
least long weekends there. He was to get to
know the locals, explain that he was a poet and,
like J. D. Salinger and Aleksandr Solzhenitsyn,
needed a retreat in New England where he
could write in solitude.

It had been clear to Milo that Jo-Jo was
reading both names and that he had no idea
who either Salinger or Solzhenitsyn was, but
the offer had come at a perfect time. His part-
time jobs were drying up. The lease on his attic
apartment was expiring, and his landlady had
flatly refused to renew it. She simply couldn't
understand why it was imperative for him to
write late at night even though he explained
that was when his thoughts transcended the
everyday world and that rap music played loud
gave wings to his poetry.

He quickly found the farmhouse in Stowe and had been living in it full-time. Even though the regular deposits to his checking account had been a lifesaver, they were not enough to support another apartment in New York. The prices were astronomical there, and Milo rued the day he had told his landlady that he needed to keep the music blasting at night so it would drown out her snoring. In short, Milo was not happy. He was sick of the country life and longed for the bustle and activity of Greenwich Village. He liked people, and even though he regularly invited some of the Stowe locals to his poetry readings, after the first couple of evenings no one came back. Jo-Jo had promised that by the end of the year he would receive a $50,000 bonus. But Milo was beginning to suspect that the farmhouse and his presence in it had something to do with Packy Noonan getting out of prison.

"I don't want to get in trouble," he warned Jo-Jo during one of his phone calls.

"Trouble? What are you talking about?" Jo-Jo had asked sadly. "Would I get my good friend in trouble? What'd you do? Rent a farm-house? That's a crime?"

A pounding on the farmhouse door inter-rupted Milo's reverie. He rushed to open it and then stood frozen at the sight of his visitors — two short, portly men in ski outfits standing in front of a flatbed with a couple of straggly-looking evergreen trees on it. At first he didn't recognize them, but then he bellowed, "Jo-Jo! Benny!" Even as he threw his arms around them he was aware of how much they had changed.

Jo-Jo had always been hefty, but he had put on at least twenty pounds and looked like an overweight tomcat, with tanned skin and bald-ing head. Benny was the same height, about five-six, but he'd always been so thin you could slip him under the door. He'd gained weight, too, and although he was only half the size of Jo-Jo, he was starting to look more like him.

Jo-Jo did not waste time. "You got a padlock on the barn door, Milo. That was smart. Open it up."

"Right away, right away." Milo loped into

the kitchen where the key to the padlock was hanging on a nail. Jo-Jo had been so specific on the phone about the size of the barn that he had always suspected it was the main reason he had been hired. He hoped they wouldn't mind that the barn had a lot of stalls in it. The owner of the farm had gone broke trying to raise a racehorse that would pay off. Instead, according to local gossip, when he went to claiming races, he invariably managed to select hopeless plugs, all of which ate to the bursting point and sat down at the starting gate.

"Hurry up, Milo," Benny was yelling even though Milo hadn't taken more than half a minute to get the key. "We don't want no local yokel to come to one of your poetry recitals and see the flatbed."

Why not? Milo wondered, but without taking the time to either grab a coat or answer his own question, he raced outside and down the field to undo the padlock and pull open the wide doors of the barn.

The early evening was very cold, and he shivered. In the fading light Milo could see that there was another vehicle behind the flatbed, a van with a ski rack on the roof. They must have taken up skiing, he thought. Funny, he would never have considered them athletes.

Benny helped him pull back the doors. Milo switched on the light and was able to see the dismay on Jo-Jo's face.

"What's with all the stalls?" Jo-Jo demanded.

"They used to raise horses here." Milo did not know why he was suddenly nervous. I've done everything they want, he reasoned, so what's with the angst? "It's the right size barn," he defended himself, his voice never wavering from its singsong gentleness, "and there aren't many that big."

"Yeah, right. Get out of the way." With an imperious sweep of his arm, Jo-Jo signaled to Benny to drive the flatbed into the barn.

Benny inched the vehicle through the doors, and then a splintering crash confirmed the fact that he had sideswiped the first stall. The sound continued intermittently until the flatbed was fully inside the barn. The space was so tight that Benny could exit only by moving from the driver's seat to the passenger seat, opening the door just enough to squeeze out, and then flattening himself against the walls and gates of the stalls as he inched past them.

His first words when he reached Milo and Jo-Jo at the door were "I need a beer. Maybe two or three beers. You got anything to eat, Milo?"

For lack of something to do when he wasn't writing a poem, Milo had taught himself to cook in his six months of babysitting the farm. Now he was glad that fresh spaghetti sauce was in the refrigerator. He remembered that the Como twins loved pasta.

Fifteen minutes later they were sipping beer around the kitchen table while Milo heated his sauce and boiled water for the pasta. To Milo's dread, listening to the brothers talk as he bustled around the kitchen, he heard the name "Packy" whispered and realized that the farmhouse indeed had something to do with Packy Noonan's release.

But *what*? And where did *he* fit in? He waited until he put the steaming dishes of pasta in front of the twins before he said point-blank: "If this has something to do with Packy Noonan, I'm out of here now."

Jo-Jo smiled. "Be reasonable, Milo. You rented a place for us when you knew we were on the lam. You've been getting money deposited in your bank account for six months. All you have to do is sit here and write poetry, and in a couple of days you get fifty thousand bucks in cash and you're home free."

"In a couple of days?" Milo asked, incredulous, his mind conjuring up the happiness that $50,000 could buy: A decent place to rent in the Village. No worry about part-time jobs for at least a couple of years. No one could make a buck last as long as he could.

Jo-Jo was studying him. Now he nodded with satisfaction. "Like I said, all you need to do is sit here and write poetry. Write a nice poem about a tree."

"What tree?"

"We're just as much in the dark as you are, but we'll all find out real soon."

7

can't believe I'm sitting here having dinner with not only Alvirah and Willy but Nora Regan Reilly, the famous writer, and her family, Opal thought. This morning after watching that miserable Packy Noonan on television, I felt like turning my face to the wall and never getting out of bed again. Shows how much everything can change.

And they were all so nice to her. Over dinner they had told her about Luke being kidnapped and held hostage on a leaky houseboat in the Hudson River with his driver, who was a single mother with two little boys, and how they would have drowned if Alvirah and Regan hadn't rescued them.

"Alvirah and I make a good team," Regan Reilly said. "I wish we could put our heads together and find your money for you, Opal. You do think that Packy Noonan has it hidden somewhere, don't you?"

"Sure he does," Jack Reilly said emphatically. "That case was in the federal court, so we didn't handle it, but my guess is that guy has a stash somewhere. When you add up what the feds knew Packy spent, there's still between seventy and eighty million dollars missing. He probably has it in a numbered account in Switzerland or in a bank in the Cayman Islands."

Jack was sipping coffee. His left arm was around the back of Regan's chair. The way he kept looking at her made Opal wish that somewhere along the way she had met a special guy. He's so handsome, she thought, and Regan is so pretty. Jack had sandy hair that tended to curl, his hazel eyes were more green than brown, and his even features were enhanced by a strong jaw. When he and Regan walked into the dining room together, they were holding hands. Regan was tall, but Jack was considerably taller and had broad shoulders to match.

Even though it was only the second week in November, an early heavy snowfall had meant there was real powder on the slopes and on the ground. Tomorrow the Reillys were going to downhill ski. It was funny that Jack's name was Reilly too, Opal thought. She and Alvirah and Willy were going to take a walk in the woods and find Alvirah's tree. Then in the afternoon they were going to take lessons in cross-country skiing. Alvirah told her that she and Willy had done cross-country skiing a couple of times, and it wasn't that hard to keep your balance — and it was fun.

Opal wasn't sure how much fun it would be, but she was willing to give it a try. Years ago in school, she had always been a good athlete, and she almost always walked the mile back and forth to work to keep trim.

"You have that blank look in your eyes that says you're doing some deep thinking," Luke observed to Nora.

Nora was sipping a cappuccino. "I'm re-membering how much I enjoyed the story of the Von Trapp family. I read Maria's book long before I saw the film. It's so interesting to be here now and realize that a tree she watched being planted has been chosen for Rockefeller Center this year. With all the worries in the world, it's comforting to know that New York schoolchildren will welcome that tree. It makes it so special."

"Well, the tree is only down the road enjoy-ing its last weekend in Vermont," Luke said drily. "Monday morning before we leave, we can all go over, watch it being cut down, and kiss it good-bye."

"On the car radio I heard that they'll take it off the barge in Manhattan on Wednesday morning," Alvirah volunteered. "I think it would be exciting to be there when the tree ar-rives at Rockefeller Center. I know I'd like to see the choirs of schoolchildren and hear them sing."

But even as the words were coming from her mouth, Alvirah began to have a funny feeling that something would go wrong. She looked around the cozy dining room. People were lingering over dinner, smiling and chatting. Why did a cold certainty fill her that trouble was brewing and Opal would be caught up in it? *I shouldn't have asked her to come,* Alvirah worried. *For some reason she's in danger here.*

8

Packy's first night in the halfway house known as The Castle was not much better, in his opinion, than a step up from the federal penitentiary. He was signed in, given a bed, and once again had the rules explained to him. He immediately reconfirmed his ability to leave The Castle on Sunday morning by piously explaining that as a good Catholic he never missed Mass. He threw in for good measure the fact that it was the anniversary of his mother's death. Packy had long since forgotten exactly when his mother died, but the easy tear that rushed to his eye on cue and the roguish smile that accompanied his confession — "God bless her. She never gave up on me" — made the counselor on duty hasten to reassure him that on Sunday he could certainly attend Mass on his own.

The next day and a half passed in a blur. He dutifully sat in on the lectures warning him that he could be sent back to prison to complete his sentence if he did not follow strictly the terms of his parole. He sat at meals visualizing the feasts that he would soon be eating at fine restaurants in Brazil, sporting his new face. On Friday and Saturday night he closed his eyes in the room he was sharing with two other recently released convicts and drifted into sleep, dreaming of Egyptian cotton sheets, silk pajamas, and finally getting his hands on his flask of diamonds.

Sunday morning dawned crisp and clear. The first snowfall had occurred two weeks ago, much earlier than usual, and the forecast was that another one was on the way. It looked as if an old-fashioned winter was looming, and that was fine with Packy. He wasn't planning to share it with his fellow Americans.

Over the years of his incarceration he had managed to keep in contact with the Como twins by paying a number of carefully chosen visitors to other convicts to mail letters from him and then bring the Comos' letters to him. Only last week Jo-Jo had confirmed the arrangement to meet behind Saint Patrick's Cathedral by writing to urge him to attend the 10:15 Mass at the cathedral and then take a walk on Madison Avenue.

So Benny and Jo-Jo would be there. Why wouldn't they? Packy asked himself. At eight o'clock he closed the door of The Castle and stepped out onto the street. He had decided to walk the one hundred blocks, not because he wanted the exercise, but because he knew he would be followed and wanted his pursuer to have a good workout.

He could hear the instructions received by the guy who had been assigned to tail him: "Don't take your eyes off him. Sooner or later he'll lead us to the money he's hidden away."

No, I won't, Packy thought as he walked rapidly down Broadway. Several times, when stopped by a red light, he looked around casually as though enchanted by the world he had been missing for so long. The second time he was able to pick out his pursuer, a beefy guy dressed like a jogger.

Some jogger, Packy thought. He'll be lucky if he hasn't lost me before Saint Pat's.

On Sunday mornings the 10:15 Mass always drew the biggest crowds. That was when the full choir sang, and on many Sundays the Cardinal was the celebrant. Packy knew just where he was going to sit—on the right side, near the front. He would wait until Holy Communion was being given out and get on line with everyone else. Then, just before he received, he would cut across to the left of the altar to the corridor that led to the Madison Avenue townhouse that served as an office for the archdiocese. He remembered that when he was in high school, the kids in his class had assembled in the office and marched into the cathedral from there.

Jo-Jo and Benny would be parked in the van at the Madison Avenue entrance of the townhouse, and before the beefy guy had a chance to follow, they would be gone.

Packy got to the cathedral with time to spare and lit a candle in front of the statue of Saint Anthony. *I know if I pray to you when I've lost something, you'll help me find it,* he reminded the saint, *but the stuff I want is* hidden, *not lost. So I don't need to pray for anything that I want to find. What I want from* you *is a little help in losing Fatso the Jogger.*

His hands were cupped in prayer, which enabled him to conceal a small mirror in his palms. With it he was able to keep track of the jogger who was kneeling in a nearby pew.

At 10:15 Packy waited until the processional was about to start from the back of the church. Then he scurried up the aisle and squeezed into an end seat six rows from the front. With the mirror he was able to ascertain that four rows behind him the jogger was unable to get an end seat and had to move past two old ladies before he found space.

Love the old ladies, Packy thought. They always want to sit at the end. Afraid they'll miss something if they move over and make room for someone else.

But the problem was that there was lots of security in the cathedral. He hadn't counted on that. Even a two-year-old could see that some of those guys in wine-colored jackets weren't just ushers. Besides that, there were a few cops in uniform stationed inside. They would be all over him if he set foot on the altar.

Worried for the first time and his confidence shaken, Packy surveyed the scene more carefully. Beads of perspiration dampened his forehead as he realized his options were few. The side door on the right was his best shot. The time to move was when the Gospel was read. Everybody would be standing, and he could slip out without the jogger noticing he was gone. Then he would turn left and run the half block to Madison Avenue and up Madison to the van. "Be there, Jo-Jo. Be there, Benny," he whispered to himself. But if they were not and even if he was followed, it wasn't a parole violation to leave church early.

Packy began to feel better. With the help of the mirror he was able to ascertain that one more person had squeezed into the jogger's pew. True to form, the old ladies had stepped into the aisle to let him in, and now the jogger was cheek by jowl with a muscular kid who would not be easy to push aside.

"Let us reflect on our own lives, what we have done and what we have failed to do," the celebrant, a monsignor, was saying.

That was the last thing Packy wanted to reflect on. The epistle was read. Packy didn't hear it. He was concentrating on making his escape.

"Alleluia," the choir sang.

The congregation got to its feet. Before the last man was standing, Packy was at the side door of the cathedral that opened onto Fiftieth Street. Before the second alleluia was chanted, he was on Madison Avenue. Before the third prolonged al-le-lu-ia, he had spotted the van, opened the door, leaped into it, and it was gone.

Inside the cathedral the husky teenager had become openly belligerent. "Listen, mister," he told the jogger. "I might have knocked over these ladies if I let you shoot past me. Cool it, man."

9

On Sunday afternoon Alvirah said admiringly, "You're a natural on skis, Opal."

Opal's gentle face brightened at the praise. "I really used to be a good athlete in school," she said. "Softball was my specialty. I guess I'm just naturally coordinated or something. When I put on those cross-country skis, I felt as if I was dancing on air right away."

"Well, you certainly left Alvirah and me at the starting gate," Willy observed. "You took off as if you'd been born on skis."

It was five o'clock. The fire was blazing in their rented villa at the Trapp Family Lodge, and they were enjoying a glass of wine. Their plans to find Alvirah's tree had been postponed. Instead, on Saturday, when they learned that the afternoon cross-country lessons were all booked up, they quickly signed up for the morning instructor. Then, following lunch on Saturday, a vacancy had opened in the afternoon group, and Opal had gone off with them.

On Sunday, after Mass at Blessed Sacrament Church and an hour of skiing, Alvirah and Willy had had enough and were happy to go back to their cabin for a cup of tea and a nap. The shadows were lengthening when Opal returned. Alvirah had just started to worry about her when she glided up to the cabin, her cheeks rosy, her light brown eyes sparkling.

"Oh, Alvirah," she sighed as she stepped out of the skis, "I haven't enjoyed myself this much since—" She stopped, and the smile that had been playing around her lips vanished.

Alvirah knew perfectly well what Opal had

been about to say: "I haven't had this much fun since the day I won the lottery."

But Opal's smile had been quick to come back. "I've had a wonderful day," she finished. "I can't thank you enough for inviting me to be with you."

The Reillys—Nora, Luke, Regan, and Regan's fiancé, Jack "no relation" Reilly—had spent another long day of downhill skiing. They had arranged with Alvirah to meet at seven for dinner in the main dining room of the lodge. There Regan entertained them with the story of one of her favorite cases: a ninety-three-year-old woman who became engaged to her financial planner and was to marry him three days later. She secretly planned to give $2 million each to her four stepnieces and -nephews if they *all* showed up at the wedding.

"Actually, it was her fifth wedding," Regan explained. "The family got wind of her plan and was dropping everything to be there. Who wouldn't? But one of the nieces is an actress who had taken off on a 'Go with the Flow' weekend. She shut off her cell phone, and nobody knew where she was. It was my job to find her and get her to the wedding so the family could collect their money."

"Brings tears to your eyes, doesn't it?" Luke commented.

"For two million dollars I would have been a bridesmaid," Jack said, laughing.

"My mother used to listen to a radio program called 'Mr. Keen, Tracer of Lost Persons,'" Opal recalled. "Sounds like you're the new Mr. Keen, Regan."

"I've located a few missing people in my time," Regan acknowledged.

"And some of them would have been better off if she hadn't tracked them down," Jack said with a smile. "They ended up in the clink."

Once again it was a very pleasant dinner, Opal thought. Nice people, good conversation, beautiful surroundings—and now her newfound sport. She felt a million miles away from the Village Eatery where she had been working for the last twenty years, except for the few months when she had the lottery money in the bank. Not that the Village Eatery was such a bad place to work, she assured herself, and it's kind of an upscale diner because it has a liquor license and a separate bar. But the trays were heavy and the clientele was mostly college students, who claimed to be on tight budgets. That, Opal had come to believe, was nothing but an excuse for leaving cheap tips.

Seeing the way Alvirah and Willy lived since they won the lottery, and the way Herman Hicks had been able to use some of his lottery winnings to buy that beautiful apartment, made Opal realize all the more keenly how foolish she had been to trust that smooth-talking liar, Packy Noonan, and lose her chance for a little ease and luxury. What made it even harder was that Nora was so excited when she talked about the wedding she was planning for Regan and Jack. Opal's niece, her favorite relative, was saving for her wedding.

"I've got to keep it small, Aunt Opal," Kristy had told her. "Teachers don't make much money. Mom and Dad can't afford to help, and you wouldn't believe how much even a small wedding costs."

Kristy, the child of Opal's younger brother, lived in Boston. She had gone through college on a scholarship with the understanding that she would teach in an inner city school for three years after she graduated, and that's what she was doing now. Tim Cavanaugh, the young man she was marrying, was going to school at night for his master's degree in accounting. They were such fine young people and had so many friends. I'd love to plan a beautiful wedding for them, Opal thought, and help them furnish their first home. If only . . .

Woulda, shoulda, coulda, hada, oughta, she chided herself. Get over it. Think about something else.

The "something else" that jumped to mind was the fact that the group of six people she skied with on Saturday afternoon had passed an isolated farmhouse about two miles away. A man had been standing in the driveway loading skis on top of a van. She had had only a glimpse of him, but for some crazy reason he seemed familiar, as if she had run into him recently. He was short and stocky, but so were half the people who came into the diner, she reminded herself. He's a type, nothing more than a type; that's the long and short of it. That's why I thought I should know who he is. Still, it haunted her.

"Is that okay with you, Opal?" Willy asked.

Startled, Opal realized that this was the second time Willy had asked that question. What had he been talking about? Oh, yes. He had suggested that they have an early breakfast tomorrow, then head over to watch the Rockefeller Center tree being cut down. After that they could find Alvirah's tree, come back to the lodge, have lunch, and pack for the trip home.

"Fine with me," Opal answered hurriedly. "I want to buy a camera and take some pictures."

"Opal, I have a camera. I intend to take a picture of Alvirah's tree and send it to our broker." Nora laughed. "The only thing we ever got from him for Christmas was a fruitcake."

"A jar of maple syrup and a tree to tap hundreds of miles from where you live isn't what I call splurging," Alvirah exclaimed. "The people whose houses I cleaned used to get big bottles of champagne from their brokers."

"Those days went the way of pull-chain toilets," Willy said with a wave of his hand. "Today you're lucky if someone sends a gift in your name to his favorite charity which (a) you never heard of, and (b) you haven't a clue how much he sent."

"Luckily in my profession people never want to hear from us, especially during the holidays," Luke drawled.

Regan laughed. "This is getting ridiculous. I can't wait to watch the Rockefeller Center tree being cut down. Just think of all the people who are going to see that tree over the Christmas season. After that it would be fun to see how swift we are following the map to Alvirah's tree."

Regan couldn't possibly know that their lighthearted outing would turn deadly serious tomorrow when Opal skied off alone to check out the short, stocky man she had glimpsed at the farmhouse—the farmhouse where Packy Noonan had just arrived.

IO

I feel like I'm at the Waltons, Milo thought as he raised the lid of the big pot and sniffed the beef stew that was simmering on the stove. It was early Sunday evening, and the farmhouse actually felt cozy with the aroma of his cooking. Through the window he could see that it had started to snow. Despite the heartwarming scene he couldn't wait for this job to be finished so he could get back to Greenwich Village. He needed the stimulation of attending readings and being around other poets. They listened respectfully to his poems and clapped and sometimes told him how moved they

71

were. Even if they didn't mean it, they were good fakers. They give me the encouragement I need, he thought.

The Como twins had told Milo that they expected to be back at the farmhouse anytime after six on Sunday evening and to be sure to have dinner ready. They had left on Saturday afternoon, and if they'd seemed nervous when they arrived with the flatbed, it didn't compare to how they acted when they took off in the van. He had innocently asked them where they were going, and Jo-Jo had snapped back, "None of your business."

I told him to take a chill pill, Milo remembered, and he almost blew a gasket. Then Jo-Jo screamed at Benny to take the skis off the roof of the van and load them back again properly. He said one ski looked loose, and it would be just like Benny to load a ski that would fall off on the highway and hit a patrol car. "All we need are state troopers on our case, pawing our phony licenses."

Then fifteen minutes later he had yelled at Benny to come back inside because a bunch of cross-country skiers were passing across the field. "One of them skidding around out there could be an eagle-eyed cop," he snapped. "Your picture was on TV when they did the story on Packy, wasn't it? Maybe you want to take his bunk in the pen?"

They're scared out of their minds — that had been Milo's assessment. On the other hand, so was he. It was clear to him that wherever the twins were going involved risk. He worried that if they were arrested and talked about him, he could at the very least be accused of harboring fugitives. He shouldn't be doing business with people on the lam, and he was already sure that their little excursion had to do with Packy Noonan getting out of the can. Would anyone believe that thirteen years ago he didn't know that the twins had disappeared at the exact time Packy was arrested and that he had had nothing to do with them since? Until now, of course, he corrected himself.

No, he decided. No one would believe it.

The twins had eluded capture for years, and from the well fed look of the two of them and their new bright choppers that didn't even look fake, they had been living well. So they certainly had at least *some* of the money that the investors had lost in the scam. Why did they risk coming back? he wondered.

Packy had paid his debt to society, Milo thought, but he's still on parole. But from the way the twins were talking when they didn't think I could overhear them, it's obvious they're all planning to skip the U. S. of A. in the next few days. To where? With what?

Milo forked a chunk of beef from the stew and popped it in his mouth. Jo-Jo and Benny had stayed with him for less than twenty-four hours, but in that short time all the years they hadn't laid eyes on each other melted away. Before Jo-Jo got crabby, they had had a few laughs about the old days. And after Benny had downed a couple of beers, he had even invited him to come visit them in Bra—

At that memory Milo smiled. Benny had started to say "Bra—" and Jo-Jo had shut him up. So instead of saying "Brazil," which he clearly meant to say, Benny had said, "Bra-bra, I mean, Bora-Bora."

Benny had never been all that swift on the uptake, Milo remembered.

He began to set the table. If by chance the twins showed up with Packy Noonan, would Packy enjoy the stew, or had he gotten his fill of stew in prison? Even if he did, it wouldn't be anything like the way *I* make it, Milo assured himself. And, besides, if anyone doesn't like stew, I have plenty of spaghetti sauce. From all the stories he had heard, Packy could get pretty mean when things didn't go exactly his way. I wouldn't mind making his acquaintance, though, he admitted to himself. There is no denying that he has what they call charisma. That is one of the reasons his trial got so much coverage—people can't resist criminals with charisma.

A green salad with slivers of Parmesan cheese, homemade biscuits, and ice cream would complete the meal that would satisfy the queen of England if she happened to show up on her skis, Milo congratulated himself. These mismatched chipped dishes aren't fit for royalty, he thought, but they didn't matter. God knows it shouldn't matter to the twins. No matter how much money they got their hands on, they'd still be the same goons they always were. As Mama used to say, "Milo, honey, you can't buy class." And, boy, was she right about *that!*

There was nothing more he could do until they returned. He walked to the front door and opened it. He glanced at the barn and once again asked himself the question: What's with the flatbed? If they are headed back to Bra Bra Brazil, they sure can't be traveling there by way of a flatbed. There had been a couple of scrawny-looking spruces on the flatbed when they arrived, but yesterday Benny threw them into one of the stalls.

Maybe I should write a poem about a tree, Milo mused as he closed the door and walked over to the battered old desk in the parlor that the renting agent had the nerve to call an antique. He sat down and closed his eyes.

A scrawny tree that nobody wants, he thought sadly. It gets thrown into a horse stall, and there's a broken-down nag that is headed for the glue factory. They are both scared. The tree knows its next stop is the fireplace.

At first the tree and the nag don't get along, but because misery loves company and they can't avoid each other, they become best friends. The tree tells the nag how he never grew tall, and everyone called him Stumpy. That's why he has been plopped here in the stall. The nag tells how in the one race he could have won he sat down on the track after the first turn because he was tired. Stumpy and the nag comfort each other and plan their escape. The nag grabs Stumpy by a branch, flings him over his back, breaks out of the stall, and races to the forest where they live happily ever after.

With tears in his eyes, Milo shook his head. "Sometimes beautiful poetry comes to me full-blown," he said aloud. He sniffled as he pulled out a sheet of paper and began to write.

II

From the first moment he spotted the van on Madison Avenue, Packy Noonan realized that in thirteen years the combined brain power of the Como twins had not increased one iota. As he leaped into the backseat and slammed the door behind him, he fumed. "What's with the skis? Why not put up a sign reading Packy's Getaway Car?"

"Huh?" Benny grunted in bewilderment.

Jo-Jo was behind the wheel and stepped on the gas. He was a fraction too late to make the traffic light and decided not to risk it, especially with a cop standing at the corner. Even though the cop wasn't actually facing them, running a light was not a good idea.

"I said you should bring skis so that we could put them on after you picked me up," Packy snapped. "That way if someone noticed me hightailing it down the block, they'd say I got in a van. Then we pull over somewhere and put the skis on top. They're looking for any old van, not a van with skis. You're so dopey. You might as well plaster "Honk if You Love Jesus" stickers all over the van, for God's sake."

Jo-Jo spun his head. "We risked our necks to get you, Packy. We didn't have to, you know."

"Get moving!" Packy shrieked. "The light's green. You want a special invitation to step on the gas?"

The traffic was heavier than usual for a Sunday morning. The van moved slowly up the long block to Fifty-second Street, and then Jo-Jo turned east. Precisely the moment they were out of view, the man Packy had dubbed Fatso came running up Madison Avenue. "*Help!-*

Help! Did anybody see some guy running?" he began to yell.

The cop, who had not noticed Packy either running or getting in the van, hurried over to the jogger, clearly believing he had a nut case on his hands. New Yorkers and tourists, united for the moment in a bit of excitement, stopped to see what was going on.

The jogger raised his voice and shouted, "Anybody see where a guy went who was running around here a minute ago?"

"Keep it down, buddy," the cop ordered. "I could arrest you for disturbing the peace."

A four-year-old who had been standing across the street next to his mother while she answered a call on her cell phone tugged at her skirt. "A man who was running got into a van with skis on it," he said matter of factly.

"Mind your business, Jason," she said crisply. "You don't need to be a witness to a crime. Whoever they're looking for is probably a pickpocket. Let them find him. That's what they're paid to do." She resumed her conversation as she took his hand and started walking down the street. "Jeannie, you're my sister, and I have your best interests at heart. *Drop that creep.*"

Less than two blocks away the van was moving slowly through the traffic. In the backseat Packy willed the vehicle forward: Park, Lexington, Third, Second, First.

At First Avenue, Jo-Jo put on the turn signal. Ten more blocks to the FDR Drive, Packy fretted. He began to bite his nails, a long-forgotten habit he had overcome when he was nine. I'm not doing anything wrong until I don't show up at The Castle tonight, he reasoned. But if I'm caught with the twins, it's all over. Associating with known felons means instant parole revocation. I should have had them leave the van parked somewhere for me. But even if I was alone and got stopped, how would I explain the van? That I won it in a raffle?

He moaned.

Benny turned his head. "I got a good feeling, Packy," he said soothingly. "We're gonna make it."

But Packy observed that sweat was rolling down Benny's face. And Jo-Jo was driving so slowly that they might as well be walking. I know he doesn't want to get caught in an intersection, but this is nuts! Overhead, a thumping sound indicated that one of the skis was coming loose. "Pull over," Packy screamed. Two minutes later, between First and Second Avenues, he yanked the skis off the roof of the van and tossed them in through the back door. Then he waved Jo-Jo over to the passenger seat. "Is this the way they taught you to drive in Brazil? You, Benny, get in the back."

For the next twenty minutes they sat in dead silence as they traveled north. Benny, easily intimidated, cowered in the backseat. He had forgotten that Packy goes nuts when he's worried. So what's going on? he wondered. In those letters he told us to find somebody we could trust to rent a farmhouse with a big barn in Stowe. We did that. And then he sends word to get a two-handled saw, a hatchet, and rope, and then the flatbed. We did that. He told us to pick him up today. We did that. So what's it all about? Packy swore that he had left the rest of the loot in New Jersey, so why are we going to Vermont? I never heard of going to New Jersey by way of Vermont.

Sitting in the front seat, Jo-Jo was thinking in the same vein. Benny and I had ten million bucks with us when we took off for Brazil. We lived nice there, very, very nice, but not over the top. Packy tells us that he has another seventy or eighty million he can get his hands on once he's out of jail. But he never said how much Benny and me get in the split. If it goes sour, Benny and me could end up with Packy in the slammer. We should've stayed in Brazil and let him slave away for a few weeks at that dumpy diner where they got him a job. Then when we came to rescue him, maybe he'd appreciate us a little more. In fact, he'd be kissing our feet.

When they saw the "Welcome to Connecticut" sign, Packy let go of the wheel and clapped his hands. "One state closer to Vermont," he chortled. With a broad grin he turned to Jo-Jo. "But we're not gonna be there long. We'll take care of business and be on our way to sunny Brazil."

God willing, Jo-Jo thought piously. But something tells me that Benny and I should have made do with ten million bucks. His stomach gurgled as he made a feeble attempt to return Packy's smile.

12

At a quarter of eight Milo heard the sound of a vehicle coming up the driveway. With nervous anticipation he rushed to open the front door. He watched as Jo-Jo got out of the front passenger door of the van and Benny emerged from the door behind him.

So who's driving? he wondered. But then the question was answered as the driver's door opened and a figure appeared. The faint light from the living room window was all Milo needed to confirm his hunch that Packy Noonan was the mystery guest.

Benny and Jo-Jo waited for Packy to precede them up the porch steps. Milo jumped back to open the door as wide as possible. He felt as if he should salute, but Packy extended his hand. "So you're Milo the poet," he said. "Thanks for holding down the fort for me."

If I had known I was holding it down for you, I wouldn't be here, Milo thought, but he found himself smiling back. "It's a pleasure, Mr. Noonan," he said.

"Packy," Packy corrected him gently as his glance darted around the room. He sniffed. "Something smells real good."

"It's my beef stew," Milo told him, the words tumbling from his mouth. "I hope you enjoy beef stew, Mr.—I mean, Packy."

"My favorite. My mama made it for me every Friday—or maybe it was Saturday." Packy was starting to enjoy himself. Milo the poet was as transparent as a teenager. I *do* have a natural way of impressing people, he thought. How else would I have gotten all those dopey investors to keep pouring money into my sinkhole?

Jo-Jo and Benny were coming into the house.

Packy decided this was the moment to make sure that Milo joined their team for good. "Jo-Jo, you brought that money like I told you?"

"Yeah, Packy, sure."

"Peel off fifty of the big ones and give them to our friend Milo." Packy put his arm around Milo's shoulders. "Milo," he said, "this isn't what we owe you. This is a bonus for being a swell guy."

Fifty hundred-dollar bills? Milo thought. But he said *the big ones*. He couldn't mean fifty *thousand*, could he? *Another* fifty thousand? Milo's brain couldn't handle the thought of that much money being handed to him in cold, hard cash.

Two minutes later he could not keep his mouth closed as a grumpy-looking Jo-Jo counted out fifty stacks of bills from a large suitcase filled with money. "There are ten C-notes in each of these here piles," he said. "Count them when you're finished writing your next poem."

"By any chance have you got anything smaller?" Milo asked hesitantly. "Hundred-dollar bills are hard to change."

"Chase the Good Humor wagon down the block," Jo-Jo snapped. "What I hear, the driver carries lots of change."

"Milo," Packy said gently. "Hundred-dollar bills aren't hard to change anymore. Now let me explain our plans. We'll be out of here by Tuesday at the latest. Which means all *you* have to do is go about your business and ignore our comings and goings until we leave. And when we leave, you will be given the other fifty thousand dollars. Are you agreeable to that situation?"

"Oh, yes, Mr. Noonan—I mean, Packy. I surely am, sir." Milo could taste and feel Greenwich Village as though he were already there.

"If somebody happened to ring the bell and ask if you'd seen a flatbed around here, you'd forget that there is indeed one on the premises, wouldn't you, Milo?"

Milo nodded.

Packy looked directly into his eyes and was satisfied. "Very good. We understand each other. Now how about some dinner? We hit a lot of traffic, and your stew smells great."

13

They're not hungry, they're *starving*, Milo thought as he refilled Packy's and the twins' plates for the third time. With satisfaction he watched as his biscuits disappeared and his salad vanished. He had done so much tasting and sampling that he had hardly any appetite, which was just as well since he kept getting up and down to open yet another bottle of wine. Packy, Jo-Jo, and Benny seemed to be in a contest to see who could drink the fastest.

But the more they drank, the more they mellowed. The skis wobbling on the roof of the van suddenly seemed hilarious. The fact that four cars had rear-ended one another on route 91, causing a massive traffic jam and forcing them to drive slowly past an army of cops, sparked another round of belly laughs.

By eleven o'clock the twins' eyes were at half-mast. Packy had a buzz on. Milo had limited himself to a couple of glasses of wine. He didn't want to wake up tomorrow and forget anything that had been said. He also intended to stay sober until his money was safely under a mattress in Greenwich Village.

Jo-Jo pushed back his chair, stood up, and yawned. "I'm going to bed. Hey, Milo, that extra fifty thousand means you do the dishes." He started to laugh, but Packy thumped on the table and ordered him to sit back down.

"We're all tired, you idiot. But we have to talk business."

With a burp he didn't try to stifle, Jo-Jo slumped back into his chair. "I beg your pardon," he mumbled.

"If we don't get this right, you may be begging the governor for a pardon," Packy shot across the table.

A nervous tremor ran through Milo's body. He simply didn't know what to expect next.

"Tomorrow we're getting up real early. We'll have some coffee, which Milo will have ready."

Milo nodded.

"Then we back the flatbed out of the barn, drive to a tree a few miles from here that happens to be located on the property of a guy I worked for when I was a kid, and cut down this very special tree."

"Cut down a *tree*?" Milo interrupted. "You're not the only one cutting down a tree tomorrow," he said excitedly. He ran over to the pile of newspapers by the back door. "Here it is, right on top!" he crowed. "Tomorrow at ten A.M. the blue spruce that was selected as this year's Rockefeller Center Christmas tree is being cut down. They've been preparing it all week! Half the town will be there, and there'll be lots of media—television, radio, you name it!"

"Where's this tree?" Packy asked, his voice dangerously quiet.

"Hmmmm." Milo searched the article. "I

could really use a pair of reading glasses," he observed. "Oh, here it is. The tree is on the Pickens property. Guess there's good pickins on the Pickens property." He laughed.

Packy jumped out of his seat. "Give me that!" he yelled. He grabbed the paper out of Milo's hands. When he laid eyes on the picture of the tree—alone and majestic in a clearing—that was about to be sent to New York City, he let out a scream. "That's my tree! *That's my tree!*"

"There are a lot of nice trees around here we could cut down instead," Milo suggested, trying to be helpful.

"*Roll out the flatbed!*" Packy ordered. "*We're cutting down my tree tonight!*"

14

At eleven o'clock, just before she got into bed, Alvirah stood at the window and looked out. Most of the villas were already in darkness. In the distance she could see the silhouette of the mountains. They're so silent and still, she thought, sighing.

Willy was already in bed. "Is anything wrong, honey?"

"No, not at all. It's just that I'm such a New Yorker, it's hard to get used to so much quiet. At home the sounds of traffic and police sirens and trucks rumbling kind of blend into a lullaby."

"Uh-huh. Come to bed, Alvirah."

"But here it's so peaceful," Alvirah continued. "I bet if you walked along any of these paths right now, you wouldn't hear a sound other than a little animal scampering through the snow or a tree rustling or maybe an owl hooting. It's so different, isn't it? In New York right now there's probably a line of cars at Columbus Circle, honking their horns because the light just changed and somebody didn't step on the gas fast enough. In Stowe you don't hear a sound on the road. By midnight all the lights will be out. Everyone will be dreaming. I love it."

A gentle snore from the bed told her that Willy had fallen fast asleep.

"Let's see what's going on in the world," Nora suggested as Luke unlocked the door to their cabin. "I like to catch the news before I go to sleep."

"That's not always the best idea," Luke commented drily. "The bedtime stories on the news aren't always catalysts for sweet dreams."

"If I can't sleep in the middle of the night, I

always turn on the news," Regan said. "It helps me fall back asleep—unless, of course, there's something big going on."

Jack picked up the remote and pressed the TV button. The screen filled with the anchor desk of the Flash News Network. The coanchors were not flashing their usual sunny smiles. A tape rolled showing Packy Noonan leaving prison. "Look at this!" Jack exclaimed.

The anchor reported solemnly: "Packy Noonan, recently released from prison after serving twelve and a half years for cheating investors in his fake shipping company, left his halfway house this morning to attend Mass at Saint Patrick's Cathedral. He was being followed by a private investigator hired by the law firm that was appointed to recover the money Packy stole. But Noonan slipped out of the cathedral during the service and was seen running down Madison Avenue. When he did not return to the halfway house this evening, he officially broke his parole. We have been receiving phone calls and e-mails from outraged investors who heard this story earlier on Flash

News. They have always believed that Noonan had squirreled away their money and is on his way to collect their fortunes right now. There is a $10,000 reward for information that helps lead to Noonan's capture. If you have any information, please contact the number on your screen below."

"That guy is taking a big risk," Jack said. "He served his time, and now if he's caught he'll be thrown back in jail for breaking parole. He must have that money stashed away somewhere and doesn't want to wait the two or three years he'd spend on parole to get his millions. My guess is that he'll be out of the country in no time flat."

"Poor Opal," Nora sighed. "That's all she needs to hear. She always said the money was hidden somewhere, and if she got her hands on Packy, she'd wring his neck."

Regan shook her head. "It makes me sick to think how many investors like Opal were cheated out of money that really would have made a difference in their lives. At least when Packy was in prison, they knew he was miserable. Now they have to wonder if he's going to be living high on the hog on their dime, just thumbing his nose at them."

"I told you," Luke said. "Now everybody's worked up before it's time to go to sleep."

In spite of the situation, they all laughed. "You're terrible," Nora chided. "I just hope Opal didn't watch the news tonight. She'd never close an eye."

A few doors down, in the villa she shared with Alvirah and Willy, Opal had fallen into a dead sleep as soon as her head hit the pillow. Even though she had not heard the news about Packy's disappearance, when she began to dream, it was of him. The gates of a dreary stone prison were bursting open. Packy came running out clutching fat pillowcases in his arms. She knew they were stuffed with money—*her* money. Her lottery money. She began to chase him, but her legs wouldn't move. In her dream she became increasingly agitated. "Why won't my legs move?" she thought frantically. "I have to catch up with him." Packy disappeared down the road. Gasping for breath as she struggled to move forward, Opal woke with a start.

"Oh, my God," she thought as she felt her heart pounding. Another nightmare about that stupid Packy Noonan. As she calmed down, she thought there was something more that her subconscious was working to bring to the surface. It's going to come to me, she thought as she closed her eyes again. I know it is.

15

All my plans," Packy moaned. "Twelve and a half stinking years doing time, and every single minute I'm dreaming of getting my hands on my tree. Now this!"

From the backseat Benny leaned forward. He stuck his head between Packy and Jo-Jo "What's so special about getting your hands on that tree?" he asked. "Are you supposed to make a wish or something?"

It was pitch dark. The van was the only vehicle on the quiet country road. Packy, Jo-Jo, and Benny were on their way to case the situation on the Pickens property. As Packy had exclaimed bitterly, "For all we know the Rockefeller

Center people left a guard overnight watching the tree. Before we go lumbering over there in the flatbed, we gotta see what's going on."

"Benny, figure it out," Jo-Jo snarled. "Packy must've hid something in the tree and is worried he won't be able to get it out. It has to be our money stuck in there, Packy. Right?"

"Bingo," Packy snapped. "You should apply to be a member of the Mensa Society. You'd be a shoo-in."

"What's the Mensa Society?" Benny asked.

"It's a kind of club. You take a test. If you pass, you get to go to meetings with other people who passed, and you congratulate one another on how smart you all are. One of them was in my cell block. He was so smart that when he passed a note to the bank teller to fork over money, he wrote it on his own deposit slip."

Packy knew he was ranting as though he was out of his mind. Sometimes it was like that when he got rattled. Get your cool back, he told himself. Breathe deep. Think beautiful thoughts. He thought about money.

Outside the temperature was dropping. He could feel the slight slip of the tires as the van hit a patch of ice.

"So answer me, Packy," Jo-Jo insisted. "Our money's in that tree. You were in the can over twelve years. So why didn't you stash it in a numbered account in Switzerland or in a safe deposit box? What turned you into a squirrel?"

Packy could not prevent his voice from becoming shrill. "Let me explain. And listen real good so I don't have to repeat 'cause we're almost there." He floored the brake as he spotted a deer emerging from the bushes at the side of the road. "Get lost, Bambi," he muttered. As though it had heard him, the deer turned and disappeared.

The road was bending sharply to the right. Packy picked up speed again but more cautiously. Suppose the tree was being guarded? What then?

"So, Packy, I wanna know what's going on," Jo-Jo said impatiently.

Jo-Jo and Benny had a right to know what they were up against, Packy admitted to himself. "You two were in on the shipping scam up to your necks. The difference is that you got away with big bucks and got to spend the last twelve years in Brazil while I shared a cell with a whacko."

"We only got ten million," Benny corrected, sounding injured. "You held on to at least seventy million."

"It didn't do me any good when I was in jail. The whole time the lamebrains were giving us money to invest I was buying diamonds, unset stones, some of them worth two million each."

"Why didn't you ask us to mind them while you were in jail?" Benny asked.

"Because I'd still be waiting on Madison Avenue for you to pick me up."

"That's not nice," Benny said, shaking his head. "So I guess the diamonds are in your tree somewhere, huh? Good thing Milo mentioned the tree's going to be cut down tomorrow morning. To think we could have been a day late and a dollar short."

"You're not helping matters, Benny," Jo-Jo interrupted his brother. "Now, Packy, why did you pick this tree way up here in Vermont? You know, Jersey has a lot of nice trees, and it's much closer to the City."

"I used to work for the people who owned this property!" Packy snapped at them. "When I was sixteen, my dear old Ma got the court to send me up here on some kind of 'save-the-troubled-kid' experiment."

"What kind of job did you have up here?" Jo-Jo asked.

"Cutting down trees, mostly for the Christmas market. I was pretty good at it. I even learned how to use a crane to get the big ones that were bought for the centers of towns all over the country. Anyway, when I was afraid that the auditors were catching on to us, I took the diamonds from the safe deposit box, put them in a metal flask, and stowed them up here. I didn't think it would be thirteen years before I'd be back for them. The people who own this property planted the tree on their wedding day fifty years ago. They swore they'd never cut it down."

"That would have been bad," Benny agreed.

"With all the developments these days, it just could have happened. Ya know, in our old neighborhood, the ball field—"

"I don't want to hear about your old neighborhood!" Packy shouted. "Now here's the turn into the clearing. Keep your fingers crossed. I'll pull over, and we'll walk the rest of the way."

"Suppose there's a guard there."

"Maybe he'll have to spend the rest of the night watching us cut down a tree. Jo-Jo, give me the flashlight."

Packy opened the door of the van and got out. His blood was racing so rapidly through his veins that he didn't notice the sharp difference between the cold night air and the warmth of the van. Keeping to the side of the path, he was ready to merge into the shadows if he caught sight of anyone near the tree. Slowly he edged around the final turn, the twins following. He couldn't believe what he saw. The light snowfall allowed enough visibility to vaguely outline the scene. Packy turned on the flashlight and kept it pointed at the ground.

Next to the tree, his tree, was a flatbed. A crane was already in place, its cables looped near the top to guide the tree onto the flatbed after it was cut down. There didn't seem to be anyone around guarding it.

Jo-Jo and Benny knew enough not to say a word.

Slowly, tentatively, Packy approached the cab of the flatbed and peered inside. There was no one there. He tried the handle of the driver's door, but it was locked. Under the bumper, he thought. Nine out of ten truck drivers leave another set of keys under the bumper.

He found them and began to laugh. "This is a gift," he told the twins. "The flatbed and the crane just *waiting* for us. We're on our way to a flask full of millions of dollars' worth of diamonds, hidden somewhere in that tree. But we have to go back to the farmhouse to get the two-handled saw. Too bad one of you imbeciles didn't think to throw it in the back of the van."

"There's a power saw on the flatbed," Benny pointed out. "Why can't we use that?"

"Are you crazy? That thing would wake the dead. You guys can cut down the tree in no time while I handle the crane."

"I've got a bad back," Benny protested.

"Listen!" Packy exploded. "Your share of eighty million dollars will pay for plenty of chiropractors and masseuses. Come on, we're wasting time!"

16

Two hundred acres away, in the eighteenth-century farmhouse in the center of his property, Lemuel Pickens was finding it hard to get to sleep. Normally he and his wife, Vidya, got into bed promptly at nine-thirty and passed out. But tonight, because of the tree, they had been reminiscing about the old days, and then they dug out the album and looked at the picture of the two of them planting the tree the day they were married, fifty years ago.

We weren't spring chickens, either. Lemuel chuckled to himself. Vidya was thirty-two, and I was thirty-five. That was old in our day. But as she always said, "Lemmy, we had responsibilities. I had my mother to take care of, and you had your father. When we'd see each other in church on Sundays, I could tell you were sweet on me, and I liked that." Then Viddy's mother died. Two weeks later Pa was feeling poorly, and before you could say "Jiminy Cricket," he had passed over, too, Lemuel remembered as he gave Viddy a poke. That woman can sure snore up a storm, he thought as she turned on her side and the rumbling stopped.

We never were blessed with children, but that tree has been almost like a child to us. Lemuel's eyes moistened. Watching it grow, the branches always so even and perfect, and the touch of blue that comes out in the sunlight. It sure is the prettiest tree I've ever seen. Even the way it stands alone in the clearing. We never wanted to plant anything near it. Over the years we've put mulch around it. Babied it. It's been fun.

He turned on his side. When those people rang the door and asked if we'd let them cut down the tree for Rockefeller Center, I almost took a gun to them. But then I heard that after I turned them down they hightailed over to Wayne Covel's place and were considering his big blue spruce. Boy, did that get my goat.

Viddy and I took about two minutes to talk it over. We're not going to be here much longer to take care of our tree. Even if we have it in our will that no one can cut it down, it won't be the same after we're gone. It won't be special to anyone, but if it goes to Rockefeller Center, it will make thousands and thousands of people happy. And when it gets to New York, the schoolkids and those cute Rockettes will greet our tree and sing the songs from Maria von Trapp's movie. Funny that she came along just as we were planting it. She knew it was our wedding day, and she sang an Austrian wedding song for us and took our picture next to the tree. Then we took her picture standing in the same spot.

Lemuel sighed. Viddy is looking forward so much to going to New York City and seeing our tree come ablaze with lights. It'll be on television all over the country, and everyone will know it's our fiftieth anniversary. They even want to interview us on the *Today Show*. Viddy's so excited, she's planning to have her hair washed and set at one of those fancy salons in New York. When I heard how much it was gonna cost, I almost dropped my teeth. But as Viddy reminded me, she's only had it done twice in all these years.

I just wish I could see the expression on Wayne Covel's face when we're on the TV talking to Katie or Matt. He's as sour as a wet hen because when we went running over and said we'd let them have our tree, they dropped *his* like a hot potato.

Lemuel gave Vidya another poke. She makes more noise than a tree crashing in the forest, he thought.

17

Twenty feet up, Wayne Covel could not believe his ears. He had been standing on the ladder behind Lemuel Pickens's prize blue spruce, machete in hand, about to start hacking off branches. His intention was to make such a mess of the tree that the men sent by Rockefeller Center would come running back to him. He still hadn't decided whether or not to play hard to get, but in the end he would let them have his beautiful tree.

The *Today Show* here I come, he thought.

But then from the other side of the tree he heard footsteps approaching and realized that subconsciously he had been aware of the faint sound of a car engine a few minutes earlier. It was too late for him to climb down the ladder and escape, so he did the only thing possible: He jammed the machete into the tool belt around his waist and stood perfectly still. Maybe they'll go away quickly, he hoped. Please don't let it be guards who'll stay here all night.

What do I do? he wondered frantically. I'm a trespasser. Lem Pickens would know exactly what I was up to. My goose would be cooked.

Wayne could hear several men walking around, then moving on the far side of the tree. They were talking about diamonds hidden in the tree—millions of dollars' worth of diamonds! He almost fell off the ladder, he was concentrating so hard in his attempt to make out every word they were saying.

They had to be kidding! But they weren't— he knew it. There were diamonds hidden in a metal flask somewhere in the tree, and these guys were going to steal the tree to find the jewels.

Wayne was terrified. These weren't good guys, obviously. Could he get out of here without them seeing him? If they discovered him, they'd know he heard what they were saying. Then what? He didn't want to think about the possibilities.

"We have to go back to the farmhouse to get the two-handled saw," one of them was saying in a grouchy tone. "Too bad one of you imbeciles didn't think to throw it in the back of the van."

Thank you, God! Wayne wanted to shout. They're leaving. That'll give me time to climb down and call the cops. Maybe there'll be a reward! I'll be a hero. These guys wouldn't have hid diamonds in the tree if they got them honestly, that much he knew for sure.

He waited until he could no longer hear the sound of their car, then reached into his belt, pulled out his flashlight, and turned it on. Where could they have hidden a flask of diamonds? It had to be attached to a branch or to the trunk. The branches weren't thick enough to hold a flask inside. And if anyone had drilled a hole in the trunk, the nutrients wouldn't get through, and the tree would die.

Wayne leaned forward, lifted a few of the branches with his thick protective gloves, and shined the flashlight all around. What a joke, he thought. Talk about a needle in a haystack. But maybe I'll get lucky and spot the flask. Sure—and maybe Boston will finally win the World Series.

Even so, he descended the ladder one step at a time, carefully parting the branches and shining the flashlight between them. Three steps down, the beam of light caught on something resting on a branch above, about halfway between the trunk and the ladder.

It couldn't be—or could it?

Wayne grabbed the machete from his belt and leaned into the tree. The needles scratched his face and became embedded in his handlebar mustache, but he didn't feel them. He couldn't reach the machete far enough to cut the branch off past the object, or could he?

Wayne was on his tiptoes leaning into the tree when, with one strike, he cut the branch in half, pulled off the severed end, and scampered down the ladder. At the bottom his flashlight revealed a metal flask held tight to the branch with the kind of thin wire used in electric fences. Wayne's whole body quivered with excitement.

With a sweep of the machete Wayne cut the branch again so that the section holding the flask was only a foot long. He stifled the impulse to let out a whoop of triumph, as he did whenever the Red Sox scored a run against the Yankees, and began to run. In his haste he did not realize that the machete with his name on the handle had slid out of his belt and fallen to the ground.

All thoughts of calling the cops had vanished.

God works in strange ways, he thought as he ran around the perimeter of Lem Pickens's property. If my tree had been picked, I would have had my fifteen minutes of fame, but then it would have been over. This way, if this flask really is full of diamonds, I'm rich—and that pain in the neck Lem misses his chance to be a star.

He only wished he had the nerve to show

up the next morning and see Lem's face when he visits his tree for the last time and finds nothing but a stump. Wayne was delirious with joy. And how about seeing the faces on the guys when they discover that the branch with the flask is half gone? But he wished them luck. They were doing his job for him. If they really succeeded at cutting down Lem's tree, then his might be on its way to Rockefeller Center.

Wayne ran faster through the night. I should check my horoscope, he thought. My planets must be all lined up. They just gotta be.

18

Back at the farmhouse Milo was roused from his nap on the couch and ordered into the kitchen for a briefing from Packy.

"I don't want to get in this any deeper," Milo protested.

"You're in it up to your neck," Packy barked. "Now we've got to get this right. We can't fit two flatbeds in the barn, and we can't leave one out in sight."

"There are plenty of lonely roads around here," Benny noted. "Why don't we leave ours on one of them? Although it's a shame—it was a good buy. Right after you sent word from prison to buy an old flatbed, Jo-Jo and I came

119

across that one at an auction. Paid cash for it, too. We were so proud of ourselves."

"Benny, please!" Packy yelled. "When we get back here with my tree, you'll pull our flatbed out of the barn, drive north on route 100 for about ten miles, and lose it somewhere. No. Wait a minute! Milo, you drive the flatbed. They know you around here. There's no law against driving a flatbed. Benny, you follow in the van and drive him back."

This is more than I bargained for, Milo thought. I don't think I'll ever get to spend that money. But he decided not to protest. He was already in too deep, and he had never felt more miserable in his life.

"Okay, that's decided," Packy said briskly. "Milo, don't look so worried. We'll be out of your life soon enough." He glanced at the twins. "Come on, you two. We don't have that much time."

When they got back to the site, the light snowfall had ended and a few stars were visible through the clouds. In a way Packy was glad to see them.

It meant that he didn't need more than the lowest setting of the flashlight to guide Jo-Jo and Benny when they were sawing the tree.

The Rockefeller Center crane was in place to receive the tree when it fell. The cables of the crane were already attached to the tree to keep it from falling away from the flatbed.

I was nuts to think I could cut anything this big and count on its landing on our flatbed, Packy admitted to himself. I was nuts to forget that the bottom branches of a tree this big had to be wrapped. Let's face it, I was nuts to hide the diamonds in a tree in the first place. But the boys hired by Rockefeller Center took care of everything for me, he consoled himself. What pals.

Jo-Jo and Benny took their places on either side of the tree. They were each holding one end of the saw.

"All right," Packy directed. "This is the way you do it. Benny, you push while Jo-Jo pulls. Then, Jo-Jo, you push while Benny pulls."

"Then I push while Jo-Jo pulls," Benny confirmed. "And Jo-Jo pushes and I pull. Is that right, Packy?"

Packy wanted to scream. "Yes, that's right. Just start. Do it! Hurry up!"

Even though it was a manual saw, the sound seemed to reverberate through the woods. Seated on the crane, Packy pointed the beam of the flashlight on the base of the tree. For an instant he pointed it at the tree's back where he knew that somewhere the flask was hidden. He could see a ladder that hadn't been visible to him before and then noticed that a length of branch was lying on the ground. An uneasy feeling stirred inside him. He pointed the light back at the twins pushing and pulling.

Ten minutes passed. Fifteen.

"Hurry up," Packy urged them. "Hurry up."

"We're pushing and pulling as fast as we can," Benny panted. "We're almost done. We're almost—Timber!" he yelled.

They had severed the tree at the base of the trunk. For a moment it wavered and then, guided by Packy at the crane, the large tree was held in the air by cables and lowered in a straight line onto the flatbed. Sweat was pouring down Packy's face. How did I ever remember to do that right? he wondered. He released the cables, scrambled down from the crane, and rushed into the driver's seat of the cab of the flatbed. "Benny, you get in with me. Jo-Jo, follow in the van, like you're escorting us. Now if our luck holds . . ."

With agonizing slowness he drove the flatbed out of the clearing and onto the dirt road. He passed the east side of Lem Pickens's property, pulled on to route 108, and finally drove up Mountain Road.

A few cars passed them on 108, their occupants hopefully too tired or too indifferent to wonder what was going on. "Sometimes they transport big trees like this at night to avoid causing a traffic jam," Packy explained, more to himself than to Benny. "That's what these birds probably think we're doing if they think at all."

There was more that he was worried about than getting back to the barn undetected—that branch lying on the ground, right below the area where the flask was hidden. That side of the tree was now exposed on the top of the flatbed. He couldn't wait to start looking for his flask.

It was exactly 3 A.M. when they reached the farmhouse. Benny jumped out, ran to the barn, and opened the door. He backed out their flatbed, making an ear-splitting racket as the remaining horse stalls broke into splinters. Milo came rushing out of the house and took over the driver's seat of the flatbed from Benny. As Benny drove the van past Packy, he waved, smiled, and gave a light tap of the horn. Packy grunted while driving the stolen flatbed into the barn. As he climbed out, Jo-Jo was shutting the barn door.

"Now I look for the red line I painted around the trunk at the spot where the branch with the flask is, and we're halfway to Brazil. The way I figure it, now it should be about forty feet up."

Jo-Jo pulled out the tape measure Packy had ordered him to bring, and together they started to measure the tree from its base. Packy's throat went dry when he saw a broken branch about twenty feet up. Could this be where that piece of branch on the ground came from? he wondered. Ignoring the sharpness of the needles, he pulled the remaining branch back and then yelled as a piece of jagged wire cut his finger. His flashlight was pointed at the trunk and the red circle around the base of the broken branch.

There was no sign of a flask, only the remnants of the wire with which he had so carefully secured his treasure.

"What?" he screamed. "I don't get it! I thought my branch would be higher by now. We've got to go back! That flask must be stuck to the branch I saw lying on the ground by the ladder."

"We can't drive the flatbed out again! We gotta wait till Benny and Milo get back with the van," Jo-Jo pointed out.

"What about Milo's heap?" Packy screamed.

"He keeps those keys in his coat pocket," Jo-Jo answered. I should have stayed in Brazil and let Packy make salads at that dumpy diner, he thought for the third time that day.

19

Lem Pickens kept waking up. He was having bad dreams. He didn't know why, but he kept worrying that something would go wrong, that maybe he had made a mistake after all about giving up the tree.

Just natural, he told himself. Just natural. He had read in a book somewhere that any cataclysmic event in our lives brings fear and anxiety. It certainly doesn't seem to bother Viddy, he thought as she continued to make the depth of her slumber known to him. Right now the noise she's making is somewhere between a jackhammer and a chainsaw.

Lem tried thinking pleasant thoughts to ease his anxiety. Think of when they flip the switch and our tree is lit up in Rockefeller Center with over thirty thousand colored lights on it. Just think about *that!*

He knew why he was worried. It would be hard to watch the tree actually being cut down. He wondered if the tree was scared. At that moment he made a decision: I'll wake up Viddy extra early, and after we have a cup of coffee, we'll walk over and sit by our tree and say a proper good-bye to it.

That settled, and feeling somewhat content, Lem closed his eyes and drifted back to sleep. A few minutes later the racket from his side of the bed was still no competition for Viddy, an Olympic snorer if there ever was one.

As they slept, a tearful Packy Noonan was sitting on the stump of their beloved tree holding a machete in his hand, the beam of his flashlight pointing to the name visible on the handle: *Wayne Covel.*

20

Wayne Covel was panting when he reached his back door, the piece of Lem's branch with the crooks' flask wired to it clutched in his hand. He laid the branch on the table in his messy kitchen, poured a tall glass of whiskey to calm his nerves, and then dug the wire cutters out of his tool belt. With trembling fingers he cut the wire that held the flask to the branch and freed it.

Flasks hold only good things, he thought as he took a sip of the whiskey. This one had been just about sealed shut, there was so much sediment around it, and he tried to unscrew it. He walked over to the sink and turned on the faucet. A groaning sound was followed by a slight trickle of water that eventually turned hot. He held the flask under it until most of the sediment was washed off. It still took three powerful twists with his hands before the cap loosened.

He grabbed a greasy dish towel and rushed over to spread it on the table. He sat down and slowly, reverently, began to shake the contents of the flask onto the crowing rooster that marked the center of the raggy towel. His eyes bugged at the sight of the treasure unfolding in front of him. They weren't kidding—diamonds as big as an owl's eye, some of them the prettiest golden color, some of them with a bluish tint, one he'd swear was as big as a robin's egg. That one he had to give an extra shake to get through the mouth of the flask. His heart was beating so fast, he needed another long swig of whiskey. It was hard to believe this was happening.

I'm lucky Lorna dumped me last year, he thought. She said eight years of me was enough. Well, eight years of her was enough. Nag, nag, nag. I was just too nice to kick her butt out. She moved forty-five minutes away to Burlington. He heard she was doing some of that Internet dating. Good luck at finding that sensitive man you're after, honey, he thought.

He picked up a handful of diamonds, still not believing his luck. Maybe when I figure out how to unload some of this fancy stuff, I'll take a first-class trip and send Lorna a postcard telling her what a good time I'm having—and that I don't wish she was there.

Pleased at the thought of one-upping Lorna, Wayne got down to the business at hand. The minute Lem finds out that tree is gone, he'll be yelling that I was behind it. I know my face got scratched, so I have to figure out an excuse for how that happened. I could always say I was pruning one of my trees and lost my balance, he decided. The one thing he did well was take care of the trees on the property that he hadn't yet sold off.

The next problem was where to hide the diamonds. He began to put them back in the flask. I'm going to be under suspicion for cutting down the tree, so I gotta be real careful. I can't keep them in the house. If the cops decide to search the place, with my luck they'll find the flask.

Why don't I just do what those crooks out by the tree did? he thought. Why not hide it in one of my own trees until everything blows over and I can make a trip to the big city?

Wayne wrapped the flask with brown masking tape and then fished around in one after another of the cluttered kitchen drawers until he found the picture-hanging wire Lorna had bought in a forlorn attempt to beautify the house. Five minutes later he was climbing the old elm tree in his front yard and, using the crooks' fine example, he returned the flask of diamonds to the protection of Mother Nature.

21

After her nightmare about Packy, Opal could barely sleep. She woke up again and again during the night, glancing at the clock at 2:00 A.M., at 3:30, and then an hour later.

The nightmare had really been upsetting and had brought to the surface all the anger and resentment she felt toward Packy Noonan and his accomplices. She had tried to make a joke of it, but it was just so *insulting* for Packy to say that he would give 10 percent of his earnings in the diner to pay back his victims!

He's making fools of us again, she thought.

The television coverage of his release kept

running through her mind. On one of the stations they had done a quick review of the scam and showed Packy with those idiots Benjamin and Giuseppe Como, better known as Benny and Jo-Jo, at their indictments. Opal remembered sitting across a conference table from the three of them when they were urging her to invest more money. Benny had gotten up to help himself to more coffee. He moved like such a shlump—as though he had a load in his pants, as my mother used to say.

That was it! Opal thought. She quickly sat up in bed and turned on the light. She had suddenly realized that the man she had spotted putting skis on the rack of the van in front of a farmhouse when she was cross-country skiing the other day reminded her of Benny.

The group of skiers she was with on Saturday afternoon had been following the instructor, but the trail they were on had such a large group of slowpokes ahead of them that the instructor had said, "Let's try going around them this way." They ended up skiing through the woods near a shabby old farmhouse.

My shoelace broke, Opal remembered, so I sat on a rock, still in the woods but closer to the house. In front of it a man was putting skis on top of a van. He seemed familiar, but then somebody called him and he moved away. Even though he was hurrying, he seemed to shlump back into the house.

He was short and stocky. He shlumped. I'd swear now it was Benny Como!

But that's impossible, Opal told herself, her mind racing. What would he be doing up here? The district attorney who was going to prosecute the Comos at their trial said he was sure that Benny and Jo-Jo had skipped the country when they were out on bail. Why would Benny be in Vermont?

There was no staying in bed. Opal got up, put on her robe, and went downstairs. The great room was one open space with a beamed ceiling, stone fireplace, and large windows that looked out on the mountains. The kitchen area was two steps up from the rest of the room and defined by a breakfast bar. Opal made a pot of coffee, poured herself a cup, and stood at the window sipping the special Vermont brew. But she barely tasted it. As she looked out at the beautiful landscape, she wondered if Benny could possibly still be out there at that farmhouse.

Alvirah and Willy won't be up for a couple of hours, she thought. I could ski over to the farmhouse now. If that van is outside, I'll copy down the license plate number. I'm sure Jack Reilly could check it out for me.

Otherwise we'll just go watch the Rockefeller Center tree being cut down, visit Alvirah's maple syrup tree, and then go home. And I'll always wonder if that man was Benny and I missed a chance to get him locked up.

I'm not going to let that happen, Opal decided. She went upstairs and dressed quickly, putting on a heavy sweater under the ski jacket she had bought at the gift shop in the lodge. When she stepped outside, she saw that the sky was overeast and felt a damp chill in the air. More snow on the way, she thought—all the diehard skiers must be in seventh heaven to have snow this early in the season.

I have a pretty good sense of direction, she told herself as she stepped into her skis and mentally reviewed the way to the farmhouse. I won't have any trouble finding it.

She pushed off with her poles and began to ski across the field. It's so quiet and peaceful, she thought. Even though she had barely slept, Opal felt awake and alert. This might be crazy, she admitted to herself, but I need to feel as if I haven't overlooked a chance to catch those thieves and see them in handcuffs.

Leg irons, too, she added. That would be a sight to behold.

She was moving uphill at a steady pace. I'm pretty darn good on these, she thought proudly. Wait till we're having breakfast and I tell Alvirah what I was doing this morning! She'll be mad as heck at me for not waking her up.

Half an hour later Opal was in the wooded area across from the farmhouse. I have to be careful. People get up early in the country, she reminded herself—not like some of her neighbors in the city whose drawn shades were never snapped up before the crack of noon.

But there was no activity at all around the farmhouse. The van was parked directly at the front door. Any closer, and whoever was driving would have gotten out in the living room, Opal thought. She waited for twenty minutes. There wasn't a sign of anyone getting up to milk cows or feed chickens. I wonder if they have animals in the barn, she thought. It really is big. It looks as if it would hold all the animals on Noah's ark.

She skied to the left to try to get a look at the license plate on the van. It was a Vermont plate, but from where she was standing, it was impossible to make out the numbers on it. It would be taking a risk, but she had to get closer.

Opal took a deep breath, skied out of the woods and into the clearing, and didn't stop until she was a few feet from the van. I've got to make this fast and get out of here, she thought. Now very nervous, she whispered the numbers on the green and white plate. "BEM 360. BEM 360," she repeated. "I'll write it down when I'm out of sight."

*   *   *

Inside the farmhouse, at the very table where only hours before conviviality had reigned, three hungover, tired, and angry crooks were trying to figure out how to recover the flask of diamonds that had been their ticket to lifelong easy living. The machete with Wayne Covel's name engraved on the handle was in the center of the table. The local phone book was open to the page where Covel's name and phone number had been circled by Packy. Covel's address was not listed.

Milo had already made two pots of coffee and two batches of pancakes with bacon and sausage. Packy and the twins had devoured the breakfast but now ignored his cheerful suggestion: "One more batch of pancakes for growing boys?"

All three were casting malevolent stares at Covel's machete.

Might as well rustle them up, Milo thought, as he began to spoon batter into the pan. Their bad fortune had obviously not affected their appetites.

"Milo, forget the Magic Chef routine," Packy ordered. "Sit down. I've got plans for you."

Milo obeyed. Intending to turn off the pan-cakes, he instead flipped the flame under the frying pan that was brimming with bacon grease.

"You're sure you know where this crook Covel lives?" Packy asked accusingly.

"Yes, I do," Milo confirmed proudly. "It's in the second page of that article I showed you about the tree. It said how unusual it was to find two trees worthy of Rockefeller Center in the same state, never mind on neighboring property. Everybody knows where Lem Pickens lives, and Covel's right next door."

Benny wrinkled his nose. "What's burning?"

They all looked over at the stove. Flames and smoke were rising from the ancient cast-iron frying pan full of grease. Next to it the pan-cakes were rapidly turning black.

"You trying to kill us?" Packy screamed. "This place stinks!" He jumped up. "I get asthma from smoke!" He ran to the front door, yanked it open, and hurried out onto the front porch.

Standing only a few feet away, a woman on cross-country skis was staring at the license plate on the back of the van.

Her head jerked around, and their eyes locked. Even though over twelve years had passed, there was instant recognition on both their parts.

Opal turned and in a futile effort to escape pushed down hard on her poles, but in her haste she slipped and fell. Instantly, Packy was on her, his hand firmly covering her mouth, his knee on her back, holding her down. A moment later, dazed and terrified, she felt other hands grab her roughly and drag her into the house.

22

Alvirah awakened at 7:15 with a sense of anticipation. "It feels like the beginning of the holiday season, doesn't it, Willy?" she asked. "I mean, to be seeing the Rockefeller Center Christmas tree here in its natural setting, before it's all lit up in New York."

After forty years of marriage, Willy had long since become used to Alvirah's early-morning observances and had learned to grunt approval of them even as he savored the last few minutes of drowsy near sleep.

Alvirah studied him. His eyes were closed, and his head was buried in the pillow. "Willy, the world has just come to an end, and you and I are dead," she said.

"Uh-huh," Willy agreed. "That's great."

No use rousing him yet, Alvirah decided.

She showered and dressed in dark gray wool slacks and a gray and white cardigan sweater set, another of Baroness Min's selections for her. She checked her appearance in the full-length mirror on the closet door. I look okay, she decided matter-of-factly. In the old days I'd be wearing purple slacks and an orange and green sweatshirt. Inside, I'm still wearing them, I guess. Willy and I haven't changed. We both like to help out other folks. He does it by fixing leaky pipes for people who can't afford plumbers. I do it by trying to straighten out situations when people are overwhelmed with problems.

She walked over to the dresser and picked up her sunburst pin with the microphone in the center and clasped it on her sweater. I want to record what people have to say when the tree is cut down, she decided. It will make a nice little story for my column.

"Honey."

Alvirah turned. Willy was sitting up in bed. "Did you say something about the end of the world?"

"Yes, and I told you we were both dead. But don't worry. We're still alive, and they called off the end of the world."

Willy grinned sheepishly. "I'm awake now, honey."

"I'll start packing while you shower and dress," Alvirah said. "We're meeting the others in the dining room for breakfast at eight-thirty. Funny, I haven't heard a sound from Opal's room. I'd better wake her up."

She and Willy were in the master bedroom suite on the main floor of the villa; Opal was upstairs in another large bedroom. Alvirah walked into the great room, caught the aroma of coffee, and spotted Opal's note on the breakfast bar. Why would Opal be up and out already? she wondered as she hurried to read the note.

Dear Alvirah and Willy,

    I left early to do some cross-country skiing. There's something I have to

check out. I'll meet you for breakfast at
the lodge at 8:30.

Love,
Opal

With growing concern, Alvirah reread the
note. Opal's a good cross-country skier, but she
doesn't know all these trails, she told herself.
They can go into pretty remote areas. She
shouldn't be out there alone. What was so important that she had to leave so early to check it
out? she wondered.

Alvirah went over to the coffeepot and
poured herself a cup. It had a slightly bitter
taste, like coffee that had been sitting on the
burner for a couple of hours. She must have
left *very* early, Alvirah thought.

While she waited for Willy to dress, she
found herself staring out at the mountains.
Heavy clouds were forming. It was a gray day.
There are so many trails out there, she thought.
It would be so easy for Opal to get lost.

It was a quarter after eight. Opal had promised to meet them at eight-thirty. It's silly to

worry, Alvirah decided. We'll all be eating a nice breakfast together in a few minutes.

Willy emerged from the bedroom wearing one of the Austrian sweaters he had bought at the gift shop. "Do you think I should learn how to yodel?" he asked, then looked around. "Where's Opal?"

"We're meeting her at the lodge," Alvirah answered. I only hope we are, she thought.

23

Regan, Jack, Nora, and Luke left their cabin at 8:20 and headed toward the lodge.

"This is so lovely," Nora sighed. "Why is it that just when you really start to relax it's time to go home?"

"Well, if you didn't agree to speak at so many luncheons, you could be as relaxed as my dearly departed clients," Luke observed drily.

"I can't believe you said that," Regan protested. "But then again, I can."

"It's hard to say no when I can help raise money for a charity," Nora defended herself.

"The event tomorrow is particularly worthwhile."

"Of course it is, dear."

Jack had listened to the exchange with amusement. Luke and Nora have so much fun together, he thought. This is the way Regan and I will be when we've been married a long time. As he put his arm around her, she smiled up at him and rolled her eyes. "This is an ongoing dialogue," she commented.

"Let's see what you two end up talking about in thirty years," Luke said. "I guarantee you it won't be fascinating. Couples do tend to return to the same few favorite topics of conversation."

"We'll do our best to keep it interesting, Luke," Jack promised with a smile. "But I hardly think that there's anything dull about the two of you."

"Sometimes dull is preferable," Nora commented as Luke opened the door of the lodge. "Especially when I know that Regan is in potential danger because of the case she's working on."

"It's a concern I very much share," Jack said.

"That's why I'm so glad you're getting married," Nora said. "Even when you're not together, I have the feeling that you're watching out for her."

"You bet I am," Jack answered.

"Thanks, guys," Regan said. "It's nice to know I have a team of worriers behind me."

They walked through the lobby and into the dining room. A breakfast buffet was set up on a long table at one end of the room.

The hostess greeted them cheerfully. "I have your table ready. Your friends aren't here yet." She picked up menus and led them to the table. As they sat down, she said, "I understand you're leaving us today."

"Unfortunately, yes," Nora said, "but first we're going over to watch the Rockefeller Center tree being cut down."

"Too late."

"What?"

"You're too late."

"Did they do it earlier than expected?" Nora asked.

"I'll say. Lem Pickens went over to say good-bye to his tree at six o'clock this morning, and *he* was too late. It was gone. Someone cut it down in the middle of the night, and they even stole the flatbed that was supposed to take the tree to New York. Everybody's talking about it. One of the guests just said she was watching Imus on MSNBC, and he's onto the story."

"I can only imagine what Imus has to say about this," Regan commented.

"Imus said it must have been done by a bunch of drunks," the hostess reported as she handed out the menus. "He wondered who else would bother."

"It's the sort of stunt kids would pull," Jack said.

"What are they going to do now?" Nora asked the hostess.

"If they can't find the tree today, they'll probably go back to the guy who lives next door to Pickens. His tree was their second choice."

"*There's* a motive," Jack suggested, only partly in jest.

"You better believe it," the hostess replied,

her eyes wide with excitement. "Lem Pickens was already on the local news this morning, screaming that he thought his neighbor was responsible."

"He could get sued for that," Regan noted.

"I don't think he cares. Oh, look, here are your friends."

Alvirah and Willy had spotted them and were heading toward the table. Regan had the immediate impression that even though Alvirah was smiling, she seemed anxious. That feeling was confirmed when, after a quick "good morning," Alvirah asked, "Isn't Opal here yet?"

"No, Alvirah," Regan answered. "Wasn't she with you?"

"She left this morning to go cross-country skiing and said she'd meet us at breakfast."

"Alvirah, sit down. I'm sure she'll be along in a few minutes," Nora said comfortingly. "Besides, you wouldn't believe the news around here."

"What news?" Alvirah asked eagerly.

As Alvirah and Willy sat down, Regan could

see that Alvirah perked up with the prospect of hearing some dirt.

"Someone cut down the Rockefeller Center tree in the middle of the night and disappeared with it."

"*What?*"

"Nobody took Alvirah's tree, did they?" Willy asked. "Then they'd really be in trouble."

Alvirah ignored him. "Why on earth would anyone go to all that trouble to steal a tree? And where could they possibly take it?"

Quickly Regan filled them in on the fact that not only were the tree and the flatbed missing, but the owner of the tree, Lem Pickens, was accusing his neighbor of theft.

"As soon as we eat breakfast, I want to get over there and see for myself what's going on," Alvirah announced. She glanced at the doorway of the dining room. "I do wish Opal would hurry up and get here," she said.

Jack took a sip of the coffee that the waitress had just poured for him. "Do you know if Opal heard the news about Packy Noonan?"

"What news?" Alvirah and Willy asked in unison.

"He didn't go back to his halfway house last night, which means he's already broken his parole."

"Opal has always sworn that he had plenty of money hidden somewhere. He's probably on his way out of the country with that loot right now." Alvirah shook her head. "It's disgusting." She reached for the bread basket, examined it carefully, and decided on an apple strudel. "I shouldn't," she murmured, "but they're so good."

Alvirah's purse was on the floor beside her feet. The sudden ring of her cell phone made her jump. "I forgot to turn this off before I came into the dining room," she noted as she dove for her purse and fumbled for the phone. "Men have it so much easier. They just hook these things onto their belt and answer on the first ring—unless, of course, they're up to no good. . . . Hello . . . oh, hi, Charley."

"It's Charley Evans, her editor at *The New*

York Globe," Willy informed the others. "Dollars to doughnuts he knows about the missing tree. He's always on top of everything before it happens."

"Yes, we've heard about the tree," Alvirah was saying. "As soon as I finish breakfast, I'm going to run right over there, Charley. It's good human interest to talk to the locals. It has turned into a crime story, hasn't it?" She laughed. "I sure wish I could solve it. Yes, Willy and I can stay for an extra day or two to see what happens. I'll report back to you in a few hours. Oh! By the way, what's the latest on Packy Noonan? I just heard a minute ago that he didn't show up at his halfway house last night. My friend who lost money in his scam is up here with me."

As the others watched, Alvirah's expression became incredulous. "He was seen getting into a van with Vermont license plates on Madison Avenue?"

The others looked at each other. "Vermont license plates!" Regan repeated.

"Maybe he's the one who cut down the tree," Luke suggested. "Either it was Packy Noonan or

George Washington." His voice deepened. "Father, I cannot tell a lie. I did chop down the cherry tree."

"Our local historian strikes again," Regan said to Jack. "The difference between Packy Noonan and George Washington is that Packy wouldn't admit it even if he was caught with the ax in his hand."

"George Washington never said that anyhow," Nora protested. "Those silly stories were made up about him after he died."

"Well, I bet whoever cut down that tree will never become president of the United States," Willy remarked.

"Don't count on it," Luke mumbled.

Alvirah snapped closed her cell phone. "I'll turn the ringer off and put it on vibrate. Maybe Opal will call if she's running late." Placing the phone on the table, she continued, "A priest at Saint Patrick's noticed a van with Vermont license plates standing in front of the rectory on Madison Avenue. Then a mother called in and said her little boy claimed he saw a man run up the block and get into that van. Of course

Packy had just been at Mass at Saint Patrick's. The detective who was following him said he even lit a candle in front of the statue of Saint Anthony."

"Maybe the detective should light a candle there himself to help him find Packy," Willy suggested. "My mother was always praying to Saint Anthony. She was always losing her glasses, and my father could never find the car keys."

"Saint Anthony would have made a great detective," Regan commented in the same dry tone that was Luke's trademark. "I should have a picture of him in my office."

"We'd better eat," Nora suggested.

All through breakfast Alvirah kept glancing at the door, but there was no sign of Opal. The phone vibrated in Alvirah's hand as they were walking out of the dining room. It was her editor again.

"Alvirah, we just dug up some background on Packy Noonan. When he was about sixteen, he worked in a troubled youth program in Stowe, Vermont, cutting down Christmas trees for Lem Pickens. There might be no connection, but as I just told you, he *was* seen leaving New York in a van with Vermont plates. I can't imagine why he'd be bothered cutting down a tree, but keep this in mind when you're talking to people."

Alvirah's heart sank. Opal was an hour late, and there was a chance that Packy Noonan was in the area. Opal had gone to check something out. The sixth sense Alvirah could always rely on told her that there was a connection.

And it wasn't a good one.

24

🌿

Earlier that morning, as the sun was coming over the mountain, Lem and Viddy, hand in hand, were trudging across their property in their snowshoes in anticipation of one last look at their beloved tree before it belonged to the world.

"I know it's hard, Viddy," Lem said. As he spoke, his breath was visible in the early morning chill. "But let's just think of all the fun we're going to have in New York. And the tree isn't gone forever, Viddy. I hear that after they take it down, they sometimes use these trees to make chips for the Appalachian Trail."

As Viddy teetered along, she replied with tears in her voice, "Well, that's nice, Lem, but I'm not up for a hike on the Appalachian Trail. Those days are long since gone."

"Sometimes they use the tree trunks to make horse jumps for the U.S. Equestrian Center."

"I don't want any horses jumping over my tree. Where is the Equestrian Center, anyway?"

"Someplace in New Jersey."

"Forget it. This trip to New York will be the last time I pack a suitcase. When we get back from New York, you can give my bags to Goodwill and take a deduction."

They turned the bend into the clearing, and their mouths dropped. Where their beloved tree had been growing and thriving for fifty years, there was only a ragged foot-high stump. The ladder the workmen had used in preparing the tree for the trip to New York City was lying on its side, and the angle of the crane was different from the night before.

"They sneaked in early and cut down our

tree," Lem raged. "Wait till I get my hands on those New York people. It was our tree until ten A.M. this morning. They didn't have the right to cut it down a minute before."

Viddy, always the quicker of the two to process information, pointed to the crane. "But, Lemmy, why would they do this when they knew there were going to be a lot of reporters and television cameras? Everybody in New York loves publicity. Remember we read about that?" Shocked out of her earlier sentimental state, she declared, "This just doesn't make sense."

As they moved closer to the stump, they heard the sound of a vehicle approaching.

"Maybe they're coming back for the crane," Lem said as they stood protectively on either side of the stump. "I'm going to give those folks a piece of my mind."

A man in his thirties whom Lem had met yesterday when they were tying up the bottom branches of the tree was coming toward them. Phil something was his name, Lem remembered. They watched as a shocked expression came over his face. "*What happened to the tree?*" he yelled.

"You don't *know?!*" Lem exploded.

"Of course I don't know! I woke up early and decided to come on over. The others will be here by eight o'clock. And where's our flatbed?"

Viddy exclaimed, "Lem, I told you it didn't make sense for those Rockefeller Center people to cut our tree down early. But who else would have done it?"

Next to her, her husband straightened up to his full height, which had shrunk to six feet one, pointed through the woods with an accusatory finger, and bellowed, "That no good skunk Wayne Covel did this!"

Almost four hours later, when the Meehans and the Reillys arrived on the scene, Lem was still sputtering that accusation for all the world to hear. Because word had already gone out that somebody had managed to make off with a three-ton tree, the expected crowd of one hundred had grown to three hundred and counting. The woods were swarming with reporters, television cameras, and stringers from the major networks. To the delight of the assembled media, what had begun as a feel-good piece of Americana had turned into a major news story.

The Meehans and Reillys made their way to the police captain at what appeared to be the command post at the edge of the clearing. Alvirah was scanning the crowd in the hope that Opal might have gone directly there if she was running late.

Jack introduced himself and the others and told the captain that Alvirah was writing a story for a New York newspaper. "Can you bring us up to date, Chief?"

"Well, this tree that was supposed to end up in your neck of the woods got swiped. We found a flatbed abandoned on route 100, near Morristown, which I think may have been involved in the crime. They're tracing the registration. The Rockefeller Center people have offered a $10,000 reward for the tree if it's still in good condition. With all this coverage," he pointed to the cameras, "you're going to have a lot of people on the lookout for that tree."

"Do you think it might be kids who did this?" Alvirah asked.

"They would have to be darn smart kids," the Chief said skeptically. "You don't just go and chop down a tree that size. Cut it at the wrong angle, and it could fall on you. But who knows? It could turn up on a college campus full of tinsel, I suppose. I doubt it, though."

Lem Pickens was finally calming down. He had not left the spot for nearly four hours, except for his rushed trip with the police to bang on Wayne Covel's door at twenty of seven. Even Lem's righteous wrath could not keep him warm any longer. Viddy had gone back and forth to the house a couple of times to get a cup of coffee and warm up. Now, as they walked past the police chief, they stopped.

"Chief, has anyone spoken to that low-down tree-napper Wayne Covel again?"

"Lem," the Chief began wearily, "you know that there's nothing to ask him now. We routed him out of bed this morning. He denies knowing anything. Just because you think he's responsible doesn't *make* him responsible."

"Well, who else would do this?" Lem demanded. By now it was a rhetorical question.

Alvirah seized the moment. "Mr. Pickens, I'm a reporter for *The New York Globe*. Could I possibly ask you about someone who worked for you years ago?"

Lem and Viddy turned and focused on the group.

"Who did you say you were?" he asked.

"We're all from New York, and you'd be interested to know that between us all, we've solved a lot of crimes." Alvirah introduced the group to the Pickenses.

"I read your books, Nora!" Viddy exclaimed. "Why don't you all come up to the house for a cup of hot chocolate, and we'll talk."

Wonderful, Alvirah thought. We'll be able to ask about Packy Noonan without interruption.

"Yeah, come on," Lem said gruffly, confirming the invitation with a wave of his sinewy hand.

Alvirah turned to the police chief. "My friend went out cross-country skiing early this morning and was supposed to meet us for breakfast. I'm getting concerned."

Willy interrupted. "Honey, I'm sure she's fine. I'll wait here. She's bound to come along. We'll catch up with you or meet you back here."

"Do you mind?"

"No. There's a lot of action going on around here. Maybe you should give me your pin to wear."

Alvirah smiled. "That'll be the day." She fell in step with the others as they followed the Pickenses to the family homestead.

25

❧

pal had fainted as she was dragged into the house. The men laid her on a lumpy couch in the living room. She came to immediately, then realized it was better to act as if she was still unconscious until she could figure out what to do. The house smelled of burning grease, the windows and doors were open in an obvious attempt to get rid of the odor, and a cold draft made Opal shiver. Through narrowed eyes she could see that Benny and Jo-Jo must have been the ones to help Packy drag her inside.

Those three crooks all together again! Moe, Larry, and Curly, she thought disdainfully.

God didn't bless those twins with good looks, that's for sure, she thought. I remembered Benny shlumped, and now here I am. I should have told Alvirah where I was going and why. And then she had a chillier thought: What are they going to do to me?

"You can close the windows now," Packy barked. "It's freezing in here." He came over to the couch and looked down at Opal. He started to pat her on the face. "Come on, come on. You're all right."

Repulsed by his touch, Opal's eyes flew open. "Get your hands off me, Packy Noonan! You miserable thief!"

"It seems like you've come to your senses," Packy grunted. "Jo-Jo, Benny, bring her into the kitchen and tie her to a chair. I don't want her making a dash for it."

Opal's cross-country skis were on the floor. The twins hustled her into the kitchen, where a nervous Milo was making another pot of coffee and wondering what the penalty for kidnapping was. The windows in the kitchen were still open. The smell of bacon grease and charred pancakes combined with the cold air made everything seem so much worse to Opal.

She looked at Milo. "Are you the short-order cook around here? If so, it looks as if you could use a few lessons."

"I'm a poet," Milo answered unhappily.

Benny and Jo-Jo wrapped a rope around Opal's legs and torso.

"Leave my hands free," she snapped. "You might want me to write another check. And I'd like a cup of coffee."

"She's a stand-up comedienne," Jo-Jo grunted.

"No, Jo-Jo," Benny smiled. "She's a sit-down comedienne." He started to laugh.

"Shut up, Benny," Packy ordered as he came into the kitchen. "I don't see anybody else out there. She must have come alone." He sat down across the table from Opal. "How did you know we were here?"

"Give me my coffee first." Shock and then anger had been Opal's initial reactions to what had happened. She read the desperation in

Packy's face and realized that he was supposed to be at the halfway house in New York. She was sure he didn't get a weekend pass to Vermont. Was he up here to get his hands on the money she had always suspected he had hidden, and then get out of the country fast? Was the money up here somewhere? Why else would he and the Como twins have come to Vermont? Certainly not to ski.

"Milk and sugar in your coffee?" Milo asked politely. "We have two percent or skim."

"Skim and no sugar." She looked at the twins. "It wouldn't hurt you two to take your coffee that way." In a crazy way Opal was beginning to feel a sense of satisfaction at getting the chance to hurl insults at these men who had caused her so much misery. *I should be more afraid*, she thought. *But I feel as if they've already done the worst to me.*

"I've been trying to diet," Benny said, "but it's hard when you're under stress."

"You've been under stress for four days. Try twelve and a half years in the can," Packy shot back.

172

Milo placed a mug of coffee in front of Opal. "Enjoy," he whispered kindly.

"Now talk, Opal," Packy demanded.

Opal had been silently debating how much information she should give him. If she told him that someone would surely come looking here for her, would they leave her or take her with them? She decided to stay close to the truth. "When I was cross-country skiing the other day, I saw a man in the yard here putting skis on the roof of the van. He seemed familiar. I couldn't get it off my mind, and this morning I realized he reminded me of Benny so I decided to check the license plate. That's it."

"Benny strikes again," Packy growled. "Who'd you tell?"

"No one. But the people I'm with are going to start wondering why I haven't come back." She decided not to say that the friends she was with included the head of the NYPD's Major Case Squad, a licensed private investigator, and the best amateur detective on this side of the Atlantic.

Packy stared at her. "Turn on the television,

Benny," he ordered. There was a ten-inch set on the kitchen counter. "Let's see if they've discovered the stump in the woods yet."

His timing was perfect. The camera zoomed in on an agitated and furious Lem Pickens pointing at the stump on the ground and swearing that his neighbor Wayne Covel had done this to him. Packy picked up the machete on the table with Wayne's name on it.

"Yup. He's our guy," Packy said flatly. "Benny, Jo-Jo, I need to speak to you inside." He jerked his head toward Milo. "Keep an eye on her. Recite a poem or something."

"Someone cut down the Rockefeller Center tree!" Opal exclaimed as the three of them filed into the living room and huddled in the corner, out of earshot.

Milo pointed to the living room. "*They* did. Can you believe it?"

"Jo-Jo," Packy said, "did you get the sleeping pills for the flight back to Brazil?"

"Sure, Packy."

"Where are they?"

"In my bag."

"Bring me the bottle right now."

Benny looked bothered. "Packy, I know we didn't get any sleep last night. I know you're nervous and upset. But I don't think you should take a pill right now."

"*You* are an idiot," Packy said through clenched teeth.

Jo-Jo hurried upstairs and returned a moment later with the bottle of sleeping pills in his hand. He looked at Packy questioningly as he handed it to him.

"We gotta somehow get into Wayne Covel's place and find the diamonds. Even if we tie her up, there's a chance she could get away. Or if someone finds her here, she could talk. We gotta make sure she's out of it until we board the plane and are well on our way. A couple of these will keep her quiet for at least eighteen hours."

"I thought Milo was going to stay here."

"He is. He'll be sleeping right next to her." Packy shook four pills out of the bottle.

"How are you going to make them swallow those babies?" Benny whispered.

"You pour Milo a fresh cup of coffee. Drop two of these into it and stir. He'll drink it. I'm surprised he can sit still long enough to write a poem with all the coffee he inhales. I'll be nice and fix another cup for Miss Moneybags. If she doesn't drink it, we'll move to Plan B."

"What's Plan B?"

"Shove it down her throat."

Wordlessly, they all went back into the kitchen where Opal was giving Milo a laundry list of all the people who had lost money in the scam.

"One couple invested their retirement money," she said. "And they had to sell their sweet little house in Florida. Now they're supplementing their Social Security doing odd jobs. And then there was the woman who—"

"The woman who blah, blah, blah," Packy interrupted. "It's not my fault you were all so stupid. I'd like another cup of coffee."

Milo jumped up.

"Don't bother, Milo. I'll pour it," Benny offered.

"Oh, look at this!" Packy said, pointing to

the television as he took Opal's cup and walked over to the stove.

On the screen they could see the chief of police and Lem Pickens knocking at the door of a rundown farmhouse. A reporter's voice was informing the viewers that about an hour ago the police chief insisted on accompanying an outraged Lem Pickens to Wayne Covel's home. "Pickens has been feuding on and off over the years with Covel, and Covel's prized tree was almost picked for Rockefeller Center," the reporter explained.

"I remember seeing that dump when I was a kid," Packy said as he put Opal's cup back down next to her. "It looks even worse now."

The door opened, and a rumpled-looking man wearing a red nightshirt appeared. A heated dialogue ensued between him and Lem. Wayne Covel's face appeared in closeup. It was not a pretty sight.

"Take a look at those scratches," Packy snarled. "They're fresh. He got them from poking around the tree and stealing our flask."

"I hear you cut down that tree," Opal accused Packy. "What did you have hidden in it? Anything of mine?"

Packy looked her straight in the eye. "*Diamonds*," he said with a sneer. "A flask of diamonds worth a fortune. One of them is worth three million bucks. That's the one I named after you." He pointed to the television. "Scratchy stole them. But we're getting them back. I'll think of you when we're living it up on your money."

"You'll never pull this off," Opal spat.

"Yes, we will." He looked at her half-empty coffee cup and smiled. He looked over at Milo's, which was still three-quarters full. He sat down. "Now everyone be quiet. I want to watch the news."

They sat through several commercials, then the local weather report came on.

"It's gray and cold out there. It looks like more storm clouds will be moving in on us today," the weatherman warned.

Packy and Jo-Jo looked at each other. They had called their pilot in the middle of the night and told him to get to the airstrip just outside

Stowe and wait. Now with a possible storm coming, their getaway could be delayed. Packy was about to jump out of his skin, but he knew he had to sit still until the sleeping pills started to do their magic. He could feel the window of opportunity for his escape to Brazil rapidly closing on him.

When the weatherman finished his report, there was more rehashing about the stolen tree. Finally, a new segment was being introduced. "Packy Noonan, a convicted scam artist who broke parole, was seen yesterday getting into a van in Manhattan. The van had skis on the roof and Vermont license plates." Packy's mug shot flashed on the screen. "So maybe he's heading our way," the anchor suggested.

"Let's hope not," his coanchor trilled. "It's amazing that he conned so many people. He doesn't look that smart."

"He isn't," Opal said drowsily.

Packy ignored her as he jumped up to lower the volume. "Great. We can't use the van, and now my mug has been seen by people all over town."

"And nobody forgets a pretty face," Opal said. Her eyes felt so heavy.

Benny began to yawn. He looked down at the mug of coffee he was holding in his hand, and a horrified look came over his face. He turned and saw that Packy and Jo-Jo were staring at him, equally horrified. Even Benny knew better than to say anything.

Jo-Jo mouthed the words "You dope" and hurried upstairs to fetch two more sleeping pills. He came down and refilled Milo's cup.

Within twenty minutes there were three comatose figures in the farmhouse kitchen. All their heads were resting on the old wooden table.

"I'm sorry my brother Benny got distracted by the news story," Jo-Jo apologized. "Sometimes it's hard for him to focus on more than one thing at a time."

"I *know* what happened," Packy snarled. "Let's drag the poet and the mouth upstairs and tie them to the beds. Benny we'll stick in the trunk of Milo's car. As soon as we get those diamonds, we're out of town fast."

"Maybe we should leave Benny a note and come back and pick him up," Jo-Jo suggested.

"I'm not running a car pool! He'll be fine in the trunk. I just hope we don't have to carry him onto the plane. Now let's move it!"

26

The four Reillys and Alvirah sat in the parlor of Lem and Viddy's farmhouse. Over the fireplace, in identical frames, were a picture of Lem and Viddy on their wedding day planting the now missing blue spruce and another of a smiling Maria von Trapp pointing to the sapling.

Lem carried in a tray laden with cups of steaming hot chocolate. Viddy was following with a platter of homemade cookies in the shape of Christmas trees. "I just learned how to make these. I was going to give them out today when they cut the tree down, and if they went over big, I was going to make a batch to bring to New York." She frowned. "Now I can just throw away the recipe."

"Hold your horses, Viddy," Lem ordered. "We're getting that tree back even if I have to shoot Wayne Covel in the toes, one by one, until he tells us where he hid it."

Oh, boy, Regan thought. This guy means business.

Lem began to pass around the cups to the guests. Then he sat down on the high-backed old rocker across from the couch. That rocker looks as though it's part of him, Regan thought. She accepted one of the cookies from Viddy with a murmured thanks. Clearly Lem was ready to get down to business.

"Now, Alvirah, is that what you said your name was?"

"Yes."

"Where'd you get a name like that?"

"Same place you got a name like Lemuel."

"Fair enough. Now who did you want to ask me about?" He took a sip of his hot chocolate which was followed by a "hahhhhhhh." He looked around. "You'd better blow before you take a taste. It'll burn your tongue off."

Alvirah laughed. "My mother had a friend who used to pour her hot tea into a saucer. Her husband used to ask, 'Why not fan it with your hat?' "

"I have to admit that would have bugged me."

Alvirah laughed. "I guess he got used to it. They were married for sixty-two years. Now what I needed to ask you," she continued, "is if you remember someone named Packy Noonan who worked up here years ago in the late fall in a troubled youth program."

"Packy Noonan!" Viddy exclaimed. "He's the only one from that group who ever came back to pay a visit. The rest were a bunch of ingrates. Although, to be honest, for years I wondered if he'd been the kid who swiped the cameo pin off my dresser."

"We never had children of our own," Lem explained, "so we used to take part in that program during the busy season when people were coming up here and selecting their own trees. It did a lot of those troubled kids good. Made them feel good about themselves. Helped straighten them out."

"It didn't work for Packy Noonan," Alvirah said flatly.

"What do you mean?"

"He just got out of prison after serving more than twelve years for scamming people out of a lot of money. He broke his parole yesterday in New York City and was seen getting into a van with Vermont license plates. I was just wondering if you'd had any contact with him at all over these years."

"He went to prison twelve years ago?" Lem exclaimed.

"I can't believe it!" Viddy said. "Maybe he *did* take my pin! But he was so nice when he came back to say hello. I was thinking how well he had turned out. He was all spiffed up. When he was a kid he looked like a bum, but that day he looked like a million dollars."

"Somebody else's million," Luke said under his breath.

"Viddy, when was it that he knocked on our door?" Lem asked.

Viddy closed her eyes. "Now let me see. My memory is not as good as it used to be, but it's still pretty darn good."

They all waited.

Her eyes still shut, Viddy fumbled for her cup of hot chocolate, picked it up, blew on it, and took a dainty sip. "I remember it was springtime, and I was making pies for the bake sale we were having at church to raise money for the senior citizens center after the basement flooded. All the bingo cards were ruined. I can tell you that that was exactly thirteen and a half years ago. It was right after the big Mother's Day storm. Everyone got drenched coming out of church, and their corsages were ruined. Anyway, that week Packy showed up at the door. I invited him in, and he was so charming. He had a piece of my pie and a glass of milk. He said it reminded him of sitting with his mother, and he told me how much he missed her. He even had tears in his eyes. I asked what he was doing with himself, and he said he was in finance."

"I'll say he was in finance," Alvirah exclaimed. "Did you see him that day, Lem?"

"Lem was back in the woods doing some tree trimming," Viddy answered. "I blew the whistle I keep by the back door, and Lem came in 'cause he knew I never blow it unless it's important."

"I got down off the ladder and came in. Boy, was I surprised to see Packy."

"Why did he say he was here?" Alvirah asked.

"He told us he was passing through on business and wanted to come over and just thank us for all we had done for him. Then he saw the picture of the tree over the fireplace and asked if it was still our baby. I said, 'You betcha. Come out back with me and take a look.' And he did. He said it looked great. Then he helped me carry the ladder back to the barn. I invited him to stay for supper. He said he had to get going but would be in touch. Never heard from him again. Now I know why. The only calls you can make from prison are collect."

"I hope he doesn't pay us another visit. Next time I'll slam the door in his face," Viddy promised.

Regan and Alvirah exchanged glances.

"And that was thirteen and a half years ago?" Alvirah asked.

"Yes, it was," Viddy confirmed, her eyes now wide open.

"I can't understand why Packy Noonan would come back here," Lem wondered aloud. "What happened to the money he stole?"

"Nobody knows," Regan said. "But everyone seems to think that wherever he is right now, he's headed for the money he managed to hide."

"He didn't hit you up to invest in his phony shipping company that day?" Alvirah asked. "That was at the very time when his scam was operating at full steam."

"He didn't ask us for one red cent," Lem exclaimed. "He knew better than to try and pull one over on Lemuel Pickens!"

Alvirah shook her head. "He pulled one over on a lot of smart people. I have a friend who lost money in his scam at that very time. Even up to the day before Packy was arrested he was trying to get her to suggest some of her friends who might want to make an investment. It's surprising that he didn't try to get you to write a check. He must have been up here for something else. This friend I mentioned was supposed to meet us for breakfast this morning and never showed up. Just the thought of Packy possibly coming to Vermont and maybe even to this area has me terribly nervous."

"The only criminal you have to worry about around here," Lem bellowed, "is the one who lives next store. Wayne Covel. He cut down my tree, and he's going to pay for it!"

"Lem, hush," Viddy scolded. "Alvirah is worried about her friend."

"Would this Wayne Covel know Packy from when Packy was up here years ago?" Alvirah asked.

Lem shrugged. "Maybe. They're about the same age."

"Maybe I'll see if he'll talk to me."

"He won't talk to me!" Lem cried.

Viddy felt the need to change the subject. When Lem got worked up, it took a lot to calm him down. "Nora," she said quickly. "I just love to read. I even tried writing poetry. There's a new fellow in town here who got a few people together for poetry readings at the old farmhouse where he's staying. But he was dreadful, so I never went back. He read one of his old poems about a peach that falls in love with a fruit fly. Can you imagine?"

"He's Milo, that really weird guy with the long hair and short beard, right, Viddy?" Lem asked.

"Honey, he's not that weird."

"Yes, he is. He comes up to Vermont. Doesn't ski. Doesn't ice skate. Sits in that junky old farmhouse all day writing poetry. There's something weird there. Right, Nora?"

"Oh, well," Nora began, "sometimes it's good for a writer to get away and work in peace and quiet."

"Work? Writing about peaches and fruit flies is not work! I don't know how long he can keep that up. How does he pay the bills?"

Alvirah felt restless. She wanted to get out and see if there was any sign of Opal. "As you know, I'm working on a story for my paper about your tree. Is it all right if I call you later? Maybe by then the police will have some leads. I can't believe that an eighty-foot Christmas tree could vanish into thin air."

"Neither can I," Lem said. "And I'm going to organize a posse to find it!"

"More hot chocolate anyone?" Viddy asked.

27

Wayne Covel tried to get some sleep after he hid the flask of diamonds in the elm tree in his front yard.

But it was no use. He realized that hiding the diamonds in the tree was a dumb idea. If those Rockefeller Center people came swarming onto his property begging him to let them have his blue spruce, who knew what might happen? The tree in which he had hidden the flask wasn't far from it. Suppose some photographer got the notion to climb the elm and get a good picture of them cutting it down?

Having the flask out of his sight gave Wayne the willies.

Just before dawn he opened the door, went outside, climbed the elm, and retrieved the flask. He brought it back to bed with him, unscrewed the cap, took a quick peek at the diamonds, and then drifted off to sleep, cuddling the flask like a baby with a bottle.

When Lem Pickens came banging on the door with the police chief, Wayne jumped up and the flask went flying out of his hands. The cap went sailing through the air as the flask hit the uneven wooden floor with a thud. Diamonds scattered randomly around the atrociously untidy room and settled among the piles of dirty clothes on the floor.

Wayne answered the door in his red nightshirt and was appalled to find an array of television cameras waiting for him. His first thought was the terrifying possibility that the police chief had that search warrant he was worried about. When he realized they had only come a-calling so Lem could scream at him, Wayne screamed back and slammed the door in their faces. A man's home is his castle, he told him-self. He didn't have to take that guff from any-one. He bolted the door and raced back to his room to retrieve the diamonds. After he had sorted through his dirty clothes and was satisfied that he had all the diamonds back in the flask, he was uncharacteristically motivated to do a wash. I wish I'd thought to count my diamonds last night, but the flask looks full, he mused.

Grabbing one of the heaps of laundry, he walked to the door in the kitchen that led to the basement, pulled it open, flicked on the light, and made his way down the creaky steps, care-fully avoiding the bottom step that was broken. No wonder I don't come down here much, he thought as he breathed the dank sour smell of the musty cellar. I should get around to cleaning up this place someday, he thought, but now I can *hire* somebody to do it. First thing I ought to do is get rid of that coal bin. Pop switched to oil heat after World War II, but he never got around to getting rid of it. He just closed it off, put a door on it, and made it into a little workroom he never used.

I sure haven't used it either, Wayne thought. It would probably be easier to burn this place down and start from scratch than to clean it up. He dropped the pile of clothes on the floor in front of the washing machine, reached up to the shelf, grabbed the nearly empty box of detergent, and shook its remains into the machine. He scooped up half of the clothes, dropped them around the agitator, closed the lid, turned the dial, and went back upstairs.

His television set was on the kitchen counter next to his laptop computer. He put on a pot of coffee, flipped on the TV, and moved his computer to the table. For the rest of the morning he kept the television on, nervously flipping among the news stations, all of which seemed to be covering the story of the missing tree. He also heard over and over that Packy Noonan, a swindler who had just been paroled, had been seen getting into a van with Vermont plates and had worked in Stowe in a troubled youth program.

Packy Noonan, Wayne thought. Packy Noonan. It sounds familiar. I kind of remember that name.

At the same time Wayne was trying to educate himself on what was going on in the diamond world by visiting different Web sites. I've got to figure out where I can sell these, he thought. He came across a number of ads for appraisals. "We buy at the highest prices and sell at the lowest" seemed to be the slogan for most of the places that traded and sold diamonds. Yeah, right, Wayne thought. And yeah, I know diamonds are forever. They're a girl's best friend. They show you care. Give me a break! He smiled. Lorna would be salivating if she were here right now and got a look at these babies.

As if he had ESP or, better yet, she had ESP, he heard the click that meant a new e-mail had popped up in his box. Expecting it might be from someone who wanted him to do an odd job, he was surprised to see it was from the ex instead.

Wayne

I see you still haven't gotten rid of that red nightshirt and you're still feuding with

Lem Pickens. And I hear that if they can't find his tree, yours might be cut down for Rockefeller Center. I know you'd never steal his tree—it would be too much work! Maybe you'd take that machete I gave you for Christmas and hack off a branch or two, but that would be it. If they pick your tree and you want some company to go with you to New York, give me a call.

xoxo
Lorna

P.S. What's with the scratches on your face? It looks as though you have a lively new girlfriend—or maybe you were poking around that tree!

Wayne stared at the e-mail with disgust. Xoxo, hugs and kisses, he thought disdainfully—she's just looking for a free trip to New York. Wants to get in on the act. If she only knew what the really big news was around the

Covel household, she'd come flying back on her broom.

It gave him a laugh that she made a point of reminding him about the machete she gave him for Christmas. When he had opened it, she made a big deal about getting his name engraved on it. You'd have thought it was a hunk of gold. Then, slowly but surely, a troubling possibility occurred to him.

Machete.

His tool belt had felt light when he strapped it on this morning to get the flask. When he took it off, he had tossed it on the other kitchen chair. Now he dove for it and, hoping against hope, held it up.

The machete was missing!

Did I drop it near Lem's tree last night? I was out of my bird when I found the flask, so I might not have noticed if I dropped it. What did she have to put my name on it for?

Lem couldn't have found it yet, or he would have been waving it at me this morning.

Those crooks who cut the tree—maybe

they found it. Maybe they're on the way here. Maybe they'll kill me for taking the loot.

I don't want to be here all by myself, he thought. On the other hand, if I just take off, everyone will think I cut down the tree.

The phone rang. Eager to hear the sound of another voice, Wayne grabbed it. "Hello."

Whoever was at the other end of the phone said nothing.

"Hello," Wayne repeated nervously. "Is anybody there?"

The response was a click in his ear.

28

"He definitely has the flask," Packy reported as he closed his cell phone.

"How do you know?" Jo-Jo asked.

"I just know. Call it criminal instinct."

"It takes one to know one, huh, Packy?"

They were getting a late start. It was 10 A.M., and Packy and Jo-Jo were sitting in the decrepit brown sedan that the owner of the farm had originally kept around for his handyman and then had willingly sold to Milo. Fifteen years old, with dents in all the fenders, a rear bumper held on by ropes, and replacement parts that had been salvaged from a junkyard, it was a spectacular example of a vehicle that only a person as blissfully impractical as Milo would buy.

Between them Packy and Jo-Jo had hauled Milo and Opal to the upstairs bedrooms and tied them to the bedposts. They had tried to revive Benny by dunking and dunking his head in a sink full of cold water. Finally, they gave up, dragged Benny outside, and hoisted him into the trunk of the car. In a burst of brotherly love, Jo-Jo ran back inside and grabbed a pillow to place under Benny's head and a quilt to cover him. Then he closed Benny's hand over a flashlight and pinned a note to his jacket just in case he woke up and wondered what was going on.

"I wrote that he should stay put and keep quiet until we got back," Jo-Jo explained.

"Why don't you read him a bedtime story?" Packy growled.

Packy knew there was no way they could use the van even though Jo-Jo warned him that Milo complained the car wasn't too reliable.

"Maybe you can't hear what they're saying on television," Packy yelled. "They're all talking about me getting in a van with a ski rack and Vermont plates. They're saying I worked up here in Stowe when I was a kid. Every cop in Vermont, especially in this area, is taking a long, hard look at a van with ski racks. We go out in the van, and we might as well turn ourselves in and collect the reward for finding me."

"We go out in that heap, and we're lucky if we get as far as the barn," Jo-Jo retorted.

"Maybe we should go in the flatbed with the tree on it."

Packy and Jo-Jo glared at each other. Then Packy said, "Jo-Jo, we've got to get our diamonds. That guy Covel has to have them. Nobody's looking for us in this heap. Let's go."

Packy was behind the wheel. He put on his dark glasses. "Give me one of the ski hats," he snapped.

"Do you want the blue with the orange stripe or the green with the—"

"Just give me a hat!"

Packy turned on the ignition. It sputtered and died. He pumped the gas. "Come on! Come on!"

"Maybe I should put a hat on Benny," Jo-Jo suggested. "There's no heat in the trunk. His hair is still damp."

"What's the matter with you?" Packy screamed. "The minute Benny falls asleep, you act dopier than Benny when Benny's at his dopiest."

Jo-Jo had the door open. "I'm putting his hat on," he said stubbornly. "Besides, his blood is thin after being in Brazil so long."

In an effort to preserve his sanity, Packy began to consider his problems and his options. Nobody will pay attention to this car, he assured himself. The poet's been tooling around in it long enough. We have to take the chance that it won't break down. At least we know Covel is home. We have to get inside that dump he lives in and make him give us the flask. It's only ten miles to the airstrip, and the pilot is waiting for us there.

Jo-Jo got back in the car.

"Hurry up," Packy barked. "We've gotta get out of here before somebody shows up looking for Sherlock Holmes."

"Who's Sherlock Holmes?" Jo-Jo asked.

"Opal Fogarty, you idiot! *The investor!*"

"Oh, *her.* That one has a temper. I don't want to be around when she wakes up and finds herself hog-tied."

Packy did not dignify that observation with a comment. He stepped on the gas and with a roar the car took off with its three occupants, two of whom were determined to recover their diamonds and the third who, if awake, would have shared that determination.

Inside the securely locked farmhouse, the burner that Jo-Jo thought he had completely turned off under the coffeepot was flickering slightly. Before the car had left the yard, the flame went out. A moment later a noxious odor slowly began to drift from the stove, an odor that warned of escaping gas.

29

The minute Alvirah saw Willy standing off by himself near the stump of Lem and Viddy's tree, her heart sank. She charged through the crowd of gawking onlookers and rushed to him. "No Opal?" she asked.

Knowing how upset Alvirah was becoming, Willy hedged. "Well, she's not here, honey, but I bet anything she's back at our villa right now, probably packing to go home and fretting about missing us at breakfast."

"She would have called my cell phone. I left a message at the villa for her. Willy, we both know that something's happened to her."

The Reillys caught up with them. From the look on Alvirah's face, Regan could tell that Opal was still among the missing. "Why don't we head to your place?" Regan suggested. "Maybe Opal got lost when she was cross-country skiing and is just getting back to the lodge."

Alvirah nodded. "Oh, how I wish. Let's keep our fingers crossed."

They walked rapidly from the clearing, which was still filled with television cameras and reporters. Before they reached the area where they had parked their cars, Alvirah's cell phone rang. Everyone held their breath while Alvirah pulled the phone out quickly to answer it.

It was Charley Evans, Alvirah's editor. "Alvirah, the story's getting bigger by the minute. It's on every one of the cable news stations. People from all over the country are sending in e-mails expressing their disgust at whoever stole the tree. The viewers say the tree represents a piece of Americana, and they want it back."

"That's good," Alvirah said halfheartedly.

All she could think about was Opal. But Charley's next statement sent chills through her.

"And as for Packy Noonan, wait till you hear this. One of his roommates at the halfway house was watching the news about the tree stolen from Stowe and Packy being seen getting into a van with Vermont plates. He called the cops and told them that Packy was talking in his sleep the other night. First he kept mumbling, 'Gotta get the flask.' "

" 'Gotta get the flask,' " Alvirah repeated. "Well, I guess he hasn't had a drink in thirteen years. He's probably been dreaming of a cocktail or two all this time."

"But it's what else he was mumbling that is really interesting," Charley continued.

"What was that?"

"He kept saying 'Stowe.' The roommate didn't think of the town until he connected Stowe with the Vermont plates this morning."

"Oh, my God," Alvirah cried. "The friend I told you about who lost money in his scam and who came up here with us is missing."

"She's *missing!*"

Alvirah could tell that Charley's antennae for a good news story had just shot up. "She never came back this morning after an early cross-country ski run. She was supposed to meet us hours ago."

"If she ran into Packy Noonan, would she recognize him?" Charley asked.

"Like the nose on her face."

"I can tell how worried you are, Alvirah. I hope she turns up soon," Charley said. "But keep me posted," he added hastily.

Alvirah told the others about Packy's nocturnal mumblings.

" 'Gotta get the flask'?" Regan questioned. "If he wanted a drink, he didn't need to use a flask. It has to mean something else."

"A lot of people use flasks to hide their liquor," Nora suggested, "so they can have a quick nip when no one is looking."

"Remember, your uncle Terry used to do that, Nora," Luke said. "No one was better at sneaking a slug than he was."

"Dad, could you wait until after I'm married to share those heartwarming family stories?" Regan asked.

"Wait till you meet the rest of my relatives," Jack said to Regan with a smile. Then he turned serious. "I do wonder what would make Packy Noonan dream about a flask."

"I'd love to know the significance of the flask for Packy," Alvirah said quickly, "but right now what really concerns me is that he was talking about *Stowe* in his sleep."

Opal was not at the villa, nor had she been there to pack her bags. Everything was the same as when Alvirah and Willy had left hours before. Alvirah's note to Opal was still on the counter.

They hurried to the lodge and inquired at the desk.

"Our friend Opal Fogarty seems to be missing," Alvirah said. "Have there been any reports of anyone injured out on the cross-country trails?"

The girl at the desk looked concerned. She shook her head. "No, but I can assure you we patrol the trails all the time. I'll notify the people at the Sports Shop to go out and start look-ing for Miss Fogarty. How long has she been gone?"

"She left our villa early this morning and had planned to meet us for breakfast at eight-thirty. That was almost three hours ago," Alvi-rah said anxiously.

"They'll get the snowmobiles out right away. If she doesn't show up soon, we'll call the Stowe Rescue Center."

Stowe Rescue Center. The very name sounded ominous to Alvirah. "Opal went out cross-country skiing the last couple of days," she told the clerk. "Would you know if the in-structors she was with on Saturday afternoon and Sunday afternoon are around? We only skied with her in the morning."

"Let me find out for you." The clerk picked up the phone, called the Sports Shop, and began to ask questions. A few moments later she hung up. "The instructor Miss Fogarty skied with yesterday said nothing unusual hap-pened when they were on the trails. The in-structor from Saturday afternoon is off today, but she certainly didn't make any reports of trouble on the trails when they came in."

"Thank you," Alvirah said. She gave her cell phone number to the clerk and asked her to please call immediately if she received any word about Opal. Then she turned to the group, all of whom were wearing somber expressions. "I certainly have no interest in visiting my maple syrup tree at this point, and I know you all have to get going. So go ahead. I'll call you as soon as Willy and I hear anything."

Regan looked at Jack. "I don't have to get back. I'll stay and help Alvirah and Willy look for Opal."

"I'm staying, too," Jack said decisively.

Nora looked frustrated. "I wish we could stay, but I have to catch a plane first thing in the morning." She shook her head. "I can't back out of this luncheon."

"Nora, don't worry," Alvirah said. "And, Regan, you and Jack don't have to stay."

"We're staying," Regan said with finality.

"Don't look so worried, honey," Willy said to Alvirah. "It's going to be all right."

"But, Willy," she cried, "there is a chance that Packy Noonan is around here somewhere. He's broken parole, and Opal is missing. If Opal and Packy crossed paths, I don't know what he'd do to her. He knows she hates his guts and would be happy to see him back in jail. By breaking parole that's just where he'd end up."

"Alvirah, do you have a picture of Opal with you?" Regan asked.

"I don't even have a picture of Willy."

"Was Opal's picture in the newspaper when she won the lottery?" Regan asked.

"Yes. That's how that idiot Packy Noonan found out she had money and decided to go after her."

"We can get her picture off the computer then and make copies to show people and ask if they've seen her," Regan said.

"Regan and I will take care of that," Jack volunteered. "Luke and Nora, I know you have to pack up and go. Alvirah and Willy, why don't we meet you back at your villa in half an hour? Then we'll start spreading Opal's face around town."

"I have such a bad feeling," Alvirah confided. "I blame myself for inviting her up here. From the minute we arrived I had a feeling something would go wrong."

It was almost as if she could smell the gas that was already seeping through the farmhouse where Opal and Milo were lying in a drug-induced sleep.

30

After the Reillys and Alvirah left the farm-house, Viddy began to collect the empty hot chocolate cups. Lem helped her carry them to the kitchen, and it was there that the reality of what had happened hit Viddy full blast. The shock at finding her tree gone hadn't really sunk in when the police and the media were swarming around. Being on television with Lem had been exciting, and then meeting up with those nice people, the Meehans and the Reillys, had been a good distraction—particularly since Nora Regan Reilly was her favorite mystery writer.

But now all she could think about was her

tree, how she and Lem had planted it on their wedding day and how Maria von Trapp had happened to come walking along the footpath, stopped to congratulate them, and agreed to have her picture taken. And then I had the nerve to ask her if she would sing that beautiful Austrian wedding song that I had heard her sing at the lodge. She was so kind, and the song was magical. I remember thinking that we'd never plant any other tree too close so that our children would be able to play in the clearing around our wedding tree.

Viddy's eyes were welling with tears as she put the cups she was holding in the sink. We were never blessed with children, and maybe it's foolish, but how we babied that tree! We measured its height every year even though somebody else had to do it for us for the last ten years because I wouldn't let Lem get up that high on the ladder anymore.

When her unexpected company came to the house, Viddy had rushed to the breakfront and taken out the cups and saucers from her cherished set of good china. She never used them except on Thanksgiving and Christmas, and then she had her heart in her mouth for fear someone would break something. Lem's nephew's wife, Sandy, was a good enough soul, but she piled dishes one on top of the other helter-skelter when she helped to clear the table. In spite of that unwanted assistance, Viddy had somehow managed to keep her china intact all these years. A few chips here and there, but nothing to get too upset about.

Knowing Viddy's feelings about her china, Lem carefully placed the cups he was carrying on top of the drainboard. Viddy went to pick them up and put them in the sink, but suddenly her eyes flooded with tears. In an involuntary gesture to brush them away, she dropped one of the cups. But before it fell into the sink where it would certainly have landed on another cup, Lem's big hand swooped under it and saved it.

"I got it, Viddy," Lem exulted. "You still have all your fancy china."

Viddy's response was to run from the kitchen into the bedroom. Then she hurried back into the parlor with their photo album. "I don't even care about my china anymore," she cried. "I know perfectly well that the minute I close my eyes for good and Sandy gets my china, she'll use it when she makes bologna sandwiches for the kids."

With trembling fingers Viddy opened the photo album and pointed to the last picture they had taken of the tree. "Our tree! Oh, Lem, I just wanted to see the expressions on people's faces when they saw it in New York City all ablaze with lights. I wanted the tree to be like a work of art with everybody admiring it and oohing and aahing over it. I wanted to have a great big beautiful picture to put right between them."

She gestured to the two photos over the fireplace. "I wanted to have a recording of the schoolchildren singing songs when our tree arrived at Rockefeller Center. Lem, we're old now. Each year when spring comes around, I wonder if I'll see another one. I know we're not going to go out in any burst of glory, but our tree was somehow going to do it for us. It was going to make us special."

"There, there, Viddy," Lem said awkwardly. "Calm down now."

Viddy ignored him, pulled a tissue out of her housedress, blew her nose, and continued. "At Rockefeller Center they keep a history of all the trees—how tall they were and how wide they were and how old they were and who donated them and whatever was special about them. A few years ago the tree was given by a convent, and they have a picture of the nun who planted it, and another picture of her fifty years later, on the day it was cut down. That's history, Lem. Our history with our tree was going to always be there for people to read about. And now our tree has probably been thrown in the woods somewhere where it will begin to rot, and *I CAN'T BEAR IT!*"

With a wail Viddy threw down the album, collapsed onto the couch, and buried her face in her hands.

Lem stared at her, dumbfounded. In fifty years he had never heard quiet, retiring Viddy say so much or show so much emotion. *I never* realized how deep she is, he thought. I can't say I like it.

Forget the posse.

He leaned down and took her face in his hands.

"Leave me alone, Lem. Just leave me alone."

"I'll leave you alone, Viddy, but first I'm going to tell you something. Listen to me. You listening?"

She nodded.

He looked into her eyes. "You stop that crying right now because I'm making you a promise. I saved your cup, didn't I?"

Sniffling, she nodded.

"Alrighty. I say that snake Covel cut down our tree. But you heard the Rockefeller Center people say that whoever took it must have used the crane to get it onto their flatbed. So that means it should be in good shape. Now maybe that skunk managed to take the tree, but he couldn't have gotten far with it. He was still in his nightshirt early this morning when I banged on his door. He could have hidden a tree by dumping it in the woods, but he can't

hide no flatbed. Our tree is around here somewhere, and I'm going to find it. I'm going to
cover every inch of this town. I'm going to walk
across any property that has a big backyard and
peek in every barn that's big enough to hold a
flatbed, and *I'm going to find our tree!*"

Lem straightened up. "As sure as my name
is Lemuel Abner Pickens, I'm not coming back
till I come back with our tree. Do you believe
me, Vidya?"

Viddy scrunched up her face. She looked
unconvinced.

"Do you believe me, Vidya?" Lem asked
again, sternly.

"I want to. Just don't get yourself arrested
trespassing on other people's property."

But Lem was already out the door.

"Or get yourself shot," she called after him.

Lem did not hear her.

Like Don Quixote, he was a man with a mis-
sion.

31

W ill you look at all these cars?" Jo-Jo snarled. "You'd think they were giving away diamonds."

"Why do you always know just the right thing to say?" Packy snapped. "They're all here gawking at that stump we left in the ground."

There was a solid line of traffic both coming and going on the road to Lem Pickens's farm. People were pulling over, parking their cars on the rough shoulder, and walking the rest of the way into the forest. It had the feeling of opening day of football season.

"I'm surprised they're not tailgating," Packy growled. "What's the big deal about that tree anyway? If they knew the real story behind it . . ."

"If they knew the real story behind it, there'd be a lot more traffic," Jo-Jo said practically.

The road was gradually curving. As they got closer to the turnoff at the dirt road, cars were parked in a solid line.

"This may be a break for us," Packy muttered as they passed the spot where they had pulled in last night.

The road continued to curve as they went another thousand feet to a wire fence that defined the property line between Lem Pickens's and Wayne Covel's acreage. A television truck was in the driveway of the ramshackle house they had seen on television when Lem Pickens had so rudely banged on Wayne Covel's door and begun shouting accusations. A group of reporters was standing around a huge tree in Covel's front yard.

"That must be the runner-up in the beauty contest," Packy stated. "If I had time, I'd chop it down."

"Too bad it didn't win," Jo-Jo said. "Then Covel wouldn't have been nosing around our tree. Look, there he is."

The front door had opened, and Wayne Covel was standing there, grinning as the cameras were turned on him.

"This works for us," Packy said quickly. "Everyone seems to be out front. We'll go in the back way."

He drove around the bend. There were a few more cars parked there. He chose a space between two cars and parallel-parked Milo's heap where it would be less noticeable than if it stood alone.

Pulling his ski hat down over his forehead as far as it would go, Packy opened the door and got out of the car. He leaned back in and picked up the paper bag that contained Wayne Covel's engraved machete. Thank God for engravers, he thought, or else we'd be whistling in the dark for the crook who made off with our flask. But why would you bother to get a machete engraved? What a loser.

With a nervous glance in the direction of the trunk, Jo-Jo got out of the car and fell in step behind Packy who darted into the woods. They made their way to the back of Wayne's farmhouse. Peering out from the protection of the trees, they could see a small barn. The door was open, and a pickup truck was parked inside it.

"What now, Packy?" Jo-Jo whispered. "You think we can get in those cellar doors?" He pointed to the rusty metal doors that slanted up from the ground and obviously led to the basement.

"First I want to disable his car in case he decides to take off before we get the diamonds. I'm gonna yank a couple of wires in that truck."

"That's a good idea, Packy," Jo-Jo said admiringly. "It's like what the nuns did in *The Sound of Music*. Remember when the nuns said to the mother superior that they had sinned?"

"Shut up, Jo-Jo. Wait here. I'll signal you when I'm finished, and we'll cut across to the basement doors."

Packy ran across the twenty feet of open field to the barn, praying to his dead mother the whole time that no one would see him. Within two minutes he had pulled up the hood, cut a few wires with Covel's machete, and closed the hood with the intense satisfaction that Covel's machete was working for him now. That thought was followed by the realization that the last time the machete had been used was to free his flask from the branch where it had been hidden for over thirteen years. He waited at the door of the barn until he was as sure as he could be that the coast was clear. He raced diagonally across the open field to the cellar doors. A padlock that looked as though it had been in place for many years came apart easily with one blow of the machete. Holding his breath, Packy leaned over and lifted one of the doors. The creak of the rusty hinges made his blood freeze. He pulled it up enough to allow him to lower himself onto the steps. Then he signaled to Jo-Jo to make a run for it.

As Packy watched in agony, Jo-Jo lumbered across the yard. Packy held the door up as Jo-Jo began to step down, but then Jo-Jo stopped. "Should I pick up the padlock?" he asked in what to him was a whisper. "I mean, if someone takes a walk around the back and sees it, they might say to themselves, 'Hey! What's this all about?' "

"Grab it and get in here!"

Packy lowered the door above Jo-Jo, and for a moment they couldn't see anything.

"This place stinks," Jo-Jo said.

"No worse than a gym, which you obviously haven't seen the inside of lately."

"I like the beach."

When their eyes adjusted, they could see one window thick with grime that offered the only light. Packy flicked on his flashlight and looked around as he carefully navigated his way across the cluttered cement floor. The washing machine was clattering.

"Who does wash at a time like this?" Jo-Jo asked. "Maybe he's cleaning the clothes he wore when he cut off the branch. Destroying the evidence, you know, Packy? That's what they do in the movies."

"I didn't know you were such a film buff," Packy snapped.

Next to the washing machine was a crudely put together walled-off section with a door. Packy opened the door and looked inside. "Here's where we hide until we're sure Covel is alone." The tiny room had a workbench and some tools lying around.

The door from upstairs opened, and a light-bulb hanging from a wire over the stairs was flicked on. Packy and Jo-Jo practically dove into the workroom as a load of dirty clothes came flying down the steps. The light flicked off, and the door was slammed shut.

Jo-Jo peered out at the laundry all over the basement floor. "That guy is some slob. And he didn't need to scare us like that."

Packy's heart was thumping. "This isn't going to be easy. We've gotta figure out whether he's alone."

They stepped out of the work area, and Packy ran the flashlight over the new load of dirty clothes that were scattered around the base of the stairs. The washing machine began to spin with the force of a tornado.

"That thing sounds like it's going to take off," Jo-Jo noted in amazement.

The door from the upstairs opened again, shocking them both. This time in their haste to get back to the protection of the workroom,

Jo-Jo tripped over one of Wayne Covel's tattered flannel shirts. He threw out his palms to soften the impact of his contact with the rough cement floor. His right hand grazed what felt like a sharp stone. With a stifled yelp he yanked up his hand and glanced down. The stone glittered. He grabbed it and, holding it tightly, scampered on his hands and knees into the workroom.

Another load of laundry had come flying down the stairs, and the door was once again slammed shut.

"I scraped my hands," Jo-Jo complained, trying to catch his breath. "But I think it might have been worth it." He opened his hand and held it up. "Take a look." Packy leaned over and shined the flashlight on Jo-Jo's chubby palm.

Packy picked up the uncut diamond he hadn't laid eyes on in nearly thirteen years and kissed it. "I'm back," Packy mumbled.

"You sure that's one of yours?" Jo-Jo asked. "I mean *ours*."

"Yes, I'm sure! It's one of the yellow ones. You might not realize it, but you're looking at two million bucks. But what did that nut case do with the rest of them?"

"Maybe we should go through the laundry," Jo-Jo suggested. "As distasteful as I find that task, it might be worth it."

"Good idea. Get started," Packy ordered. He picked up the machete. "I'll sneak up the stairs to see what I can hear. If he's alone, we're going for him now."

32

rmed with photocopies of Opal's radiantly happy face as she held up her lottery check, Regan and Jack went back to Alvirah and Willy's villa. Under Opal's picture they had printed the information that she was missing and requested anyone who had seen her or had any leads to call either Alvirah's number or the local police.

"We posted a few of these at the lodge," Regan said. "Jack and I found out what trails her group went on yesterday. We're going to walk those trails and put up her picture on trees along the way, and where there are homes nearby, we'll ring doorbells."

"And we'll be looking out for a white van with a ski rack," Jack said. "I called my office and asked them to keep me updated on anything they learn about Packy Noonan or any breaks in that case. They can't believe I was up here when the Rockefeller Center tree was stolen. I told one of my guys to keep an eye on that case as well and to keep me posted."

They were sitting in the living room of the villa, which had somehow lost its cheery warmth. Alvirah's sense that Opal was in imminent danger strengthened with every passing minute. "Opal could be anywhere," she said, the tension in her voice obvious. "She could have been forced into a car with someone. She left so early that not many people would have been outside. Willy and I will go into town and post some pictures and show them to people. We've got to get moving before it's too late. I know I said it before, but I have a feeling that Opal is in real danger and that every second counts."

"Let's check in with each other in an hour," Regan suggested. "Jack and I both have our cell phones, and you have yours."

They left the villa together. Willy and Alvirah got into their car. Jack and Regan walked to the trail where Opal had skied with her Sunday group and followed it into the woods. Today there was no one in sight. As they walked along, Regan asked, "Jack, what do you think the chances are that Opal ran into Packy Noonan?"

"She went to check something out this morning and never came back. If she saw something suspicious and Packy Noonan is in this area . . ." He raised his hands. "Who knows, Regan?"

The snow crunched under their feet as they walked side by side, shoulders touching. Their eyes darted in and out of the woods on either side of them.

"Maybe he has a friend in this area who is hiding him," Regan said. "But why? He just spent over twelve years in prison. He's paid his debt to society for that swindle. As you said last night, he's risking a lot by breaking parole. You know, Jack, it really is odd that Packy Noonan worked for Lem Pickens and Lem's tree was cut down less than twenty-four hours after

Packy broke parole and was seen getting into a van with Vermont plates. I don't know why he'd bother cutting down a tree, but it really is a little *too* coincidental, don't you think?"

Jack nodded. Deep in thought, they continued to walk along the trail, and every thousand feet or so they posted Opal's likeness on a tree. They knocked at the doors of the occasional farmhouse they passed along the way. No one recognized Opal's picture or had seen any unusual occurrence. Anyone who was home had the television on and was watching the news about Lem Pickens's missing tree.

"Those two never did get along," one woman crisply observed. "But if you want to know my opinion, Wayne Covel would never have the energy to cut down that tree then haul it out of there. Forget it! I hired him once to do some odd jobs here, and it took forever and a day for him to get them done." She invited them in for coffee, but Regan and Jack declined.

As they walked down her path and back to the cross-country trail, Regan said, "It's been just about an hour. I'll give Alvirah a call." But from Alvirah's discouraged tone it was clear even before she told them that she and Willy were having no success in finding anyone who could help.

Regan had barely closed her phone when Jack's began to ring. It was his office. Regan watched his expression change as he listened. When he closed his cell phone, he looked at Regan. "They traced the registration on the flatbed that was abandoned. It was registered to a guy who knew nothing about the tree, but it turns out his cousins, Benny and Jo-Jo Como, were part of Packy Noonan's shipping scam. And here's the kicker: They lifted Benny's fingerprints from the steering wheel."

"Oh, my God," Regan said quietly. "Maybe Opal had a run-in with him."

"Everyone thought those guys had fled the country," Jack said. "Maybe not."

"Maybe Benny's the one who picked up Packy in the van," Regan speculated. "But a flatbed? Could Packy Noonan really have been involved in the theft of the tree? Why?"

"He paid a visit to the Pickens house less than a year before he was arrested. Maybe he was looking for a hiding place for his loot. As we both know, a lot of crooks don't trust the banks or safe deposit boxes or even accounts in places like the Cayman Islands."

"He made off with millions and millions of dollars," Regan said. "It can't all be in cash. That's a lot of cash to try to hide."

"Thieves put their money in other things such as jewelry and precious stones," Jack stated. "They can be harder to trace."

"But if he hid jewelry in Lem Pickens's tree, why would he have to go to all the trouble to cut the tree down to get it?" Regan asked. "It doesn't make sense. Well, we'd better let Alvirah know. I'm sure it will be all over the news in a few minutes. Maybe her editor has called her already." Regan redialed Alvirah's number.

Alvirah had just heard the news from Charley. "Regan, we're going back to the lodge," she said. "I feel as though we're wasting our time in town. I want to talk to the desk clerk again and find out who was actually in

Opal's ski group. I just hope they all aren't gone by now. And I want to try again to reach the ski instructor who's off today."

"We'll meet you back there. We're just about at the end of this trail."

A dead-end trail, Regan thought as she hung up the phone.

33

Lem jumped in his pickup truck and roared down the driveway. The only comfort he felt was in knowing that there was a reward for his tree, which meant that a lot of people were looking for it. He didn't care if somebody else found it first and ended up with $10,000 of Rockefeller Center's money. All he wanted was his and Viddy's tree, still pretty as a picture, on its way to its glory time in New York City. He could just see the look on Viddy's face when they pulled the switch at the big ceremony and its branches lit up with thousands of lights.

Lem turned at the end of his driveway and stepped on the gas. His plan was to drive first past Wayne Covel's house and see what was going on. From there he would go from one barn to another and up some of the dead-end roads on the outskirts of town, where skiers had built homes. A lot of those people didn't start coming around until after Thanksgiving. Covel could have driven the Rockefeller Center flatbed up any one of those roads and just left it there. No one would see it for days unless they were looking for it.

He flipped on the radio. The local station was buzzing with the news about the tree.

"If I were Wayne Covel and I had nothing to do with the disappearance of that tree, I'd sue Lem Pickens for everything he's worth — every tree he has left on his property, every chicken in his barn, all the gold in his teeth," the host was saying. "In this country you can't publicly slander people and expect to get away with it. Now we have our legal expert here —"

Faintly uneasy, Lem shut off the radio. "You people don't know anything about justice," he said, spitting out the words. "Sometimes a man just has to take things into his own hands.

Viddy needs her tree. I can't be bothered waiting around for the cops to find it. And they'd probably need something stupid like a search warrant just to take a peek in somebody's barn."

He drove slowly past Wayne Covel's house. The sight of Wayne's big tree made his blood boil. If that tree ends up in Rockefeller Center instead of mine, it'll do Viddy in, he thought. Reporters were camped on Covel's driveway. He noticed that many of the people he knew from town were standing around, admiring Covel's tree. He knew some of them couldn't stand Covel but just wanted to get their faces on TV. It was a disgrace.

Around the bend he spotted the poet's car. You couldn't miss it, with that bumper tied on. He had a mind to take the air out of the tires. How dare he waste an evening of Viddy's life boring her to death with his god-awful poems? He'd even had the nerve to hand out copies of his poem about the fruit fly. Viddy said he likes to share it with anyone and everyone.

Lem kept driving. Maybe I'll go to the outskirts of town first, he decided. Even Covel wouldn't be dumb enough to leave the tree too close to his house.

For the next hour and a half Lem trespassed on property all over Stowe. He wandered into barns, opened doors, and climbed up and looked into windows if that was the only way he could check out a structure large enough to contain a flatbed. He was chased away by clucking chickens, neighing horses, and a barnyard dog that yapped at his heels as he made his escape.

By now Lem had worked up an appetite but couldn't go home. He did not want to face Viddy until he returned with the tree. He got back in his truck and turned on the radio to see if there were any updates about its whereabouts. That was when he got the news about Benny Como's fingerprints in the flatbed. He hit the steering wheel with his hand.

"Packy Noonan did this!" he cried. I knew in my gut he was up to no good when he happened to stop by thirteen years ago, he thought. But I wanted to believe that he had mended his ways. Huh! And Viddy always said she thought he swiped her cameo pin. I just hope Packy's in on this with Wayne Covel. If Covel's innocent, I'm in big trouble. Not only will Viddy be without her tree, but she won't have a roof over her head. He decided not to let himself think about it.

Lem abandoned his plan to stop for a quick lunch at the diner. I've just got to find my tree, he thought frantically.

First things first.

34

acky crouched near the top of the basement steps, fully aware that at any moment
Wayne Covel might have a third burst of do-
mesticity and send another load of wash flying
into the basement. Which means I catch it in
the face, Packy thought. But we can't wait
much longer, he decided.

His knees and back were aching. He had already been there forty minutes.

First Dennis Dolan, a reporter from some
town in Vermont, had rung the bell and been
invited by Wayne to come in and have a cup of
coffee or a beer. Dolan explained that he

wanted to do a human interest story on Wayne in case his tree ended up in Rockefeller Center.

Packy had had to endure the story of Wayne's life, including the fact that his last girlfriend, Lorna, had sent him an e-mail just this morning.

When Dolan had finally asked his last inane question and departed, Wayne went back to the kitchen and turned up the sound of the television. Machete in hand and Jo-Jo behind him armed with masking tape and rope, Packy had been about to throw open the door and pounce on Covel when a sharp rap at the front door torpedoed that plan. Covel left the kitchen to answer it, then heartily greeted someone. From the conversation, it was a drinking buddy, Jake, who had stopped by to offer moral support to him about Lem Pickens's accusation. With the door from the basement to the kitchen open a slit, Packy was privileged to hear their exchange.

"Wayne, old boy, I told those reporters that Lem's out of his bird. He just doesn't like you no how and never did. Couldn't wait to lay something like this on you, could he? I get the idea if his tree don't show up, they'll be begging you for yours. Just a little tip. In case they ask you to be on television standing next to it when it's cut down, maybe you better run off to the barber and get a haircut. I'm on my way to him now. How about you jump in the car with me?"

At that suggestion Packy almost cried in frustration. But Wayne refused the friendly overture.

"Maybe you'll skip the haircut, but if I were you, I'd trim your mustache and get a nice close shave, though with all those scratches on your face, that might get a little messy," Jake continued. "Well, I'll be on my way."

The mention of the scratches on Wayne's face made Packy tighten his grip on the machete. You got them stealing my flask, he thought.

Wayne opened the front door as he thanked his buddy for stopping by. Then, to his despair, Packy heard another voice.

"Mr. Covel, may I introduce myself? I am Trooper Keddle, an attorney specializing in litigation. May I come in?"

No, Packy agonized. No!

He felt a tug on his leg. Jo-Jo whispered, "We can't wait around here like wallflowers hoping someone will ask us for a dance, Packy. You can't see much out of that window, but I can see enough to tell that it's getting real cloudy."

"I don't need the weather report," Packy snapped. "Shut up."

The lawyer was following Wayne into the kitchen. "Sit down," Covel told him. "Get out your notebook and write this down. If you think Lem Pickens can send you over to scare me, you're nuts, and he is, too. I didn't take his tree, and he's not suing me, neither. Got that, Troopy?"

"No, no, no, no, no, Mr. Covel," Keddle soothed. "We're talking about *you* suing *him*. He's made slanderous accusations. You see, he didn't use the word *alleged*. In the legal world you can accuse somebody of just about any crime as long as you say you *allege* that someone did something. In no uncertain terms and on national television Mr. Pickens has accused you of committing a crime. Oh, dear Mr. Covel, it is the ambition of our legal firm to see you fully compensated for this insult to your integrity. You *deserve* that, Mr. Covel. Your family deserves that."

"I'm not married, and I don't like my cousins," Wayne responded. "But are you telling me that what I heard them say on the radio is right? You mean I can sue Lem for badmouthing me?" At the thought he leaned back in his chair and laughed heartily.

"You can sue him for damaging your reputation, for causing grievous pain and emotional suffering that will undoubtedly diminish your ability to adhere to your normal work schedule, for throwing your back out when you rushed out of bed to respond to his hammering at your door, for—"

"I get the picture," Wayne said. "Sounds good to me."

"Not one penny do you have to lay out. My firm first and foremost cares about justice. 'Justice for the Victim' is inscribed over the desk of all our associates."

"How many people you got in your place, Troopy?"

"Two. My mother and myself."

I never once carried a gun, Packy thought. I never had to. I'm a white-collar crook. But I'd give anything to have one now. Still, Jo-Jo's a powerhouse. He can hold Covel down. I'll swing this machete around like I'm going to use it on him, and we'll have our diamonds in two seconds flat. Covel won't take the chance that I don't mean it. But we can't take on the ambulance chaser, too. From what I can see, he's pretty hefty, and there may still be some people in the front yard. If someone hears one yell, we're cooked.

Jo-Jo was tugging on his pants again. "You say the diamond we found is worth two million?" he whispered. "Maybe we oughta settle for that."

Packy shook his head so violently that he banged it on the door.

"That door to the basement sure creaks," Wayne explained to Trooper Keddle as he pocketed Keddle's business card and got up. "Maybe with Lem's money I can get me a new one." The suggestion elicited another guffaw, which Keddle did his best to match.

But at last Keddle, with a final sales pitch about his ability to redress the wrong Wayne had suffered, was gone.

This is it, Packy thought. No more delays. He nodded to Jo-Jo. A moment later, as Wayne passed the door to the basement on his way back to the table, it flew open, and before he could do more than grunt, he was on the floor. Packy slapped tape over his mouth, and Jo-Jo yanked first his arms and then his legs back and tied them together.

"Pull down the shades in the front room, Jo-Jo," Packy ordered. "Lock the front door. Let anyone still out there get the idea that this guy's had enough company." He laid the machete down on the floor an inch from Covel's face. "You recognize it?" he asked. "I bet you do. Maybe it'll help you remember what you did with my diamonds."

He tapped Wayne on the head. "Don't even think of trying to make a noise, or you'll be eating your name off the handle. Get it?"

Wayne nodded and kept nodding.

Packy got up and hurried to the kitchen window. Standing to the side he pulled down the shade, which ended up draped over his arm. It had been tied to the roller with twine. Some handyman, he thought, and with a contemptuous glance at Wayne, he grabbed the masking tape, pulled a chair over to the window, stood on it, and began to wrap the shade around the roller with one hand and tape it with the other.

Jo-Jo had better luck pulling down the shades in the bedroom and living room, but as he was heading for the front door to lock it, the handle turned and it opened. "Wayneeeeeee, sweeteeeee," Lorna trilled as she stepped inside. "Surprise! Surprise!"

35

Opal felt the way she had when she was under the anesthesia during her appendix operation. She remembered hearing someone say, "She's coming out of it, give her more."

Someone else said: "She's had enough to knock out an elephant."

She felt the way then that she did now—as if she were in a fog or under water and trying to swim to the surface. Way back when, during the appendix operation, she remembered trying to tell them, "I'm tough. You can't knock me out easily."

That's what she was thinking *now*. When she went to the dentist, it took practically a tank of nitrous oxide to get through having her wisdom teeth extracted. She kept telling Dr. Ajong to turn up the dial, that she was still as sober as a judge.

Where do I get such high tolerance? she asked herself, vaguely aware that for some reason she couldn't move her arms. I guess they strap you down when they're operating on you, she thought as she fell back asleep.

Some time later she began to swim up to the surface again. What the heck's the matter with me? she asked herself. You'd think I'd downed five vodkas. Why do I feel this way? The possibility came to her that she was at her cousin Ruby's wedding again. The wine they had served had been so cheap that after only a couple of glasses she ended up with a hangover.

My cousin's Ruby. . . . I'm Opal. . . . Ruby's daughter is Jade. . . . All jewels, she thought drowsily. I don't feel like an opal. Right now I feel like a pebble. The Flintstones. Somebody won a prize for suggesting they call the baby Pebbles. When I told Daddy I thought Opal was a dumb name, he said, "Talk to your mother; it was her idea." Mama said that Grandpa was the one who called us his jewels and suggested the names. *Jewels.*

Opal fell asleep again.

When she opened her eyes again, she tried to move her arms and immediately knew something was wrong. Where am I? she thought. Why can't I move? I know—Packy Noonan! He saw me looking at the license plate. Those other two. They tied me up. I was sitting at the kitchen table. They bought diamonds with the money they stole from me. They stole the Christmas tree. But they don't *have* the diamonds, not yet. The man on TV, the one with the scratches on his face, has them. What was his name? Wayne . . . I was sitting at the kitchen table. What happened? The coffee tasted funny. I didn't finish it. She fell back to sleep.

Just before she woke again, she slipped into a dream in which she had forgotten to turn off a jet on the stove. In the dream she was smelling gas. As she woke, she whispered aloud, "It's not a dream. I *am* smelling gas."

36

Alvirah and Willy reached the lodge before Regan and Jack.

"The ski patrol has covered all the trails at least once," the clerk at the front desk told them. "There is no sign of her, but everyone is on the alert."

Opal's picture was prominently displayed on top of the desk. "Have a lot of people been checking out?" Alvirah asked.

"Oh, yes," the clerk said. "As you can understand, we get a lot of weekend guests. We've pointed out the picture to everyone, but unfortunately nobody so far has had any information. A few people said they remember seeing Miss Fogarty in the dining room, but that's about it."

Regan and Jack came into the lobby.

"Oh, Regan," Alvirah said. "I just *know* that Packy Noonan and Benny Como have their hands on Opal. I called the police to see if anyone reported anything, but of course no one has. They certainly would have contacted me."

Willy voiced the thought that was on all their minds. "What next?"

Alvirah turned to the clerk. "I know you left a message for the ski instructor who was working Saturday afternoon. Could you try her again?"

"Of course I can. We left several messages, on her home phone and on her cell phone, but I'll try her again. I know she's a late sleeper on her days off. Or she could be out downhill skiing. I don't think she has her cell phone with her all the time."

"Late sleeper?" Alvirah exclaimed. "It's past noon."

"She's only twenty," the clerk said with a slight smile and began to dial.

As the clerk once again started to leave a message, Alvirah commented, "I guess we're not having any luck there."

"You mentioned trying to talk to the people who were in Opal's ski group on Saturday," Jack said. "They probably have a list of those names somewhere in the computer."

"We do. I can pull that up," the clerk told him. "Give me a minute." She darted into the office around the corner from the desk.

They stood together silently as they waited. When the clerk came back out, she was holding a list with six names on it. "I know I checked out some of these people this morning, but let me look in the computer to see if any of the rest of them are still here."

The lobby door was fired open. A redheaded boy who looked to be about ten years old charged into the lobby. His remarks to his weary-looking parents who were right behind him could not be missed by anyone on the first floor of the hotel.

"I can't *believe* someone cut down that tree! I mean, how did they *do* it? Mom, can we have the pictures developed today so I can show the kids at school tomorrow? Wait until they see that stump! I want to go to New York to see whatever tree they get with all the lights on it. Can we go there during Christmas vacation? I want to take a picture of it so I can put it next to the picture of the stump."

He only stopped talking when he noticed the picture of Opal posted by the front desk. "There's that lady who was in my cross-country ski group Saturday afternoon!" Bursting with energy, he was bouncing around as he looked at the picture.

"You know this lady?" Alvirah asked. "You went skiing with her?"

"I did. She was really cool. She told me her name was Opal, and this was her first time on skis. She was really good—a lot better than another old lady who kept crossing the tips of her skis."

Alvirah decided to ignore the "old lady" remark.

"Bobby, I *told* you," the boy's father said. "Say 'elderly woman,' not 'old lady.' "

"But what's wrong with 'old lady'?" Bobby asked. "That's what that lead singer Screwy Louie calls his wife."

"When did you ski with Opal?" Alvirah asked quickly.

"Saturday afternoon."

Alvirah turned to the parents. "Were you in that group?"

They both looked embarrassed. "No," the mother said. "I'm Janice Granger. My husband, Bill, and I skied all morning with Bobby. After lunch he wanted to go out again. The instructor knows him very well and was keeping an eye on him."

"Keeping an eye on me? I was keeping an eye on Opal." He pointed to her picture.

"What do you mean, keeping an eye on her?" Alvirah asked.

"The instructor had taken us on a different trail because there was a bunch of really slow skiers ahead of us driving us all crazy. Opal had to stop and sit down to fix her shoelace because it broke. I waited for her. I had to tell her to hurry up because she kept staring at a farmhouse."

"She was staring at a farmhouse?"

"Well, some guy was putting skis on the rack on top of his van. She was watching him. I asked her if she knew him. She said no, but he seemed familiar."

"What color was the van?" Alvirah asked quickly.

He raised his eyes, bit his lip, and looked around. "I'm pretty sure it was white."

Regan, Jack, Willy, and Alvirah, now absolutely sure that the person Opal had seen was either Packy Noonan or Benny Como, were all fearing the worst.

"Where was this farmhouse?" Jack asked quickly.

"Has somebody got a map around here?" Bobby asked.

"I've got one right here," the clerk answered.

"We've been coming up here since Bobby was born," the boy's father said. "He knows his way around here better than anybody."

The clerk placed the map of the trails on the front desk. Bobby studied it. He pointed to one trail. "This is a really cool place to ski," he said.

266

"The farmhouse?" Alvirah asked. "Bobby, where is that farmhouse?"

He pointed to a spot on the map. "This is where the slowpokes were. We kind of looped around them this way. And right over here is where the elderly woman, Opal, stopped to knot the lace on her shoe."

"And the farmhouse was right there?" Regan asked him.

"Yeah. And there's a really big barn on the side of it."

"I have an idea where that is," Bill Granger volunteered.

"Can you show us the way?" Jack asked. "We can't waste any time. This is an emergency."

"Of course."

"I'm coming, too," Bobby said emphatically, his eyes wide with excitement.

"No, you're not," Janice Granger said.

"No fair! I'm the only one who knows what the farmhouse looks like for sure," Bobby insisted.

"He's absolutely right," Alvirah said firmly.

"I don't want Bobby near any trouble," Janice said.

"Could you all just lead us there then?" Jack asked. "Please. This is terribly urgent."

Bobby's parents exchanged glances. "Our car's right outside," his father said.

"Yipppeeee," Bobby cried as he ran out the lobby door ahead of them.

They all raced out to the parking lot. Jack got behind the wheel of Alvirah and Willy's car. They followed the Grangers down The Trapp Family Lodge's long winding hill on their way to the gas-filled farmhouse where a sleepy Opal was struggling to regain consciousness.

37

Resolve was one thing. Success was something else. Lem was racing everywhere but getting nowhere. His promise to Viddy to recapture their tree was looking to be as much a possibility as jumping over the moon.

Lem was now driving down Main Street. When he saw the sign for his favorite diner, he hesitated and then pulled over. His stomach was growling so loud, he couldn't think straight. A man can't think when he's hungry, Lem quickly decided. He justified his sabbatical from his quest by reminding himself that he hadn't even had breakfast. I never got back to the house till we went there with those city folk, and, good as it is, Viddy's hot chocolate can sustain a man just so far.

He got out of the truck, and a picture of a woman tacked to a lamppost caught his eye. Lem took a quick moment to study the photo of a lady holding up her winning lottery ticket. It reminded him of the time that he could have won the Vermont lottery but forgot to buy a ticket. The numbers he and Viddy always played came up that week.

Viddy was mighty cool to me for a spell, he remembered. Thank goodness it wasn't one of those real big wins. I told Viddy the taxes they take out would knock your socks off, and then the phony salesmen would start coming around bugging us about buying things we didn't need, like land in Florida that is probably nothing but a swamp filled with alligators.

There was something mulish in Viddy's makeup. She just didn't agree.

Lem's eyes narrowed. The numbers you were supposed to call if you knew anything about that Opal woman were either the police or Alvirah Meehan's.

Alvirah was at the house today. Fancy that. We're both looking for something real important to us.

Lem went into the diner and sat at the counter. Danny was working the day shift. "Lem, sorry about your tree."

"Thanks. I've got to make this fast. I'm gonna find that tree if it kills me."

"What'll you have?"

"Ham, bacon, two fried eggs, hash browns, O.J., and two slices of white toast. No butter. I'm staying away from butter."

Danny poured him a cup of coffee. Over his head and to the right, the television set was on, but the volume was low.

Lem glanced at it. A reporter was pointing to a flatbed. Lem's hearing was starting to fail him a bit. Like in the morning, if Viddy asked if he wanted more orange juice, he was likely to answer her by asking her, "What's loose?"

"Turn that sound up, Danny," Lem yelped.

Danny grabbed the remote control and hit the volume button.

"—the abandoned flatbed where the prints

of Benny Como were found was a mess. But our inside sources tell us that among the potato chip bags, gum wrappers, and fast-food boxes, investigators found something quite odd, considering who was driving that truck."

Lem leaned forward.

"A copy of a poem entitled 'Ode to a Fruit Fly' was found above the visor. The poet is unknown. His signature is impossible to decipher."

Lem jumped up as though he had touched an electric wire. "That's Milo's poem!" he cried. "And it stinks! I am some dope!" He ran out of the diner and rushed across the street to his truck.

As he started the car and jerked out of the parking space, he got madder and madder at himself. I'm a dope! he thought again. It was as plain as the nose on my face, but did I see it? No. The guy that owns the dump Milo rents made his barn bigger years ago. Thought those mules he calls racehorses would win the Kentucky Derby. But the *barn! It's big enough to hold my tree!*

38

Where is my flask?" Packy asked quietly. "Where are my diamonds?"

It was a question impossible to answer since Wayne's mouth was taped shut. Wayne and Lorna were sitting on the kitchen chairs. Like Wayne, Lorna's hands and legs were tied. After Packy warned her that one squeal would be her last, he had not bothered to tape her mouth. He figured that she was too frightened to yell, and he was right. He also figured, in case Wayne the crook started playing games, that she might know where he was likely to have hidden the diamonds.

"Wayne," Packy said, "you took the flask out

of Pickens's tree. That wasn't nice. It was my flask, not yours. I'm going to take that tape off your mouth, and if you start to yell, I'm not going to be very happy. Understand?"

Wayne nodded.

"He understands," Lorna quavered. "He really does. He may not look smart, but he really is. I always say he could have amounted to a lot if he wasn't so lazy."

"I've heard his life story," Packy interrupted. "He told it to a reporter. He even mentioned you."

Lorna spun her head. "What did you say?" she asked Wayne.

"Packy, we've got to hurry," Jo-Jo urged.

Packy glared at Jo-Jo. He had seen the fear begin to fade from Covel's eyes. The girlfriend was right. Covel wasn't dumb. Right now the brains inside his skull were working overtime, trying to figure out how to keep the diamonds. With a quick movement Packy ripped the tape off Wayne's mouth, bringing with it some of the longer hairs of his mustache.

"Ewwwwwww," Wayne moaned.

"Don't be such a baby. Millions of women pay to get that done every month. It's called waxing." Packy leaned across the table. "The flask. The diamonds. Now."

"He hasn't any diamonds," Lorna protested. "In fact, he doesn't have two nickels to rub together. If you don't believe me, look in that cigar box next to the sink. It's full of bills. Most of them are marked 'overdue.'"

"Lady," Packy said, "shut up! Covel, we want the diamonds."

"I don't have—"

"Yes, you do!" Packy growled. From his pocket he pulled out the yellow diamond they had found on the basement floor. He waved it under Covel's nose and placed it on the kitchen table.

"This was mixed up with the dirty rags you threw downstairs."

"Somebody must have dropped it. There were a lot of people in and out of here today." Covel's voice was high-pitched.

"That diamond is gorgeous!" Lorna squealed.

He's scared, but not scared enough yet not

275

to waste our time, Packy thought. He leaned across the table until his face was only an inch from Wayne's.

"I could let Jo-Jo get rough with you. And if he does, you'll talk. But I'm kind. I'm fair." He picked up the diamond and dropped it in the chest pocket of Wayne's shirt. "That little number next to your heart is worth two million dollars. It's yours if you give us the flask with the rest of them right now."

"I'm telling you, I don't know anything about them."

He's playing for time, Packy thought. Maybe he knows someone is coming back here. He picked up the machete and looked at it thoughtfully. "I guess we're out of patience, right, Jo-Jo?"

"We're out of patience," Jo-Jo confirmed grimly.

Packy raised the machete over his head and aimed it at the kitchen table. With a loud thwack it embedded itself in the wood of the table. He pulled it free.

"That's the nice machete I gave you for Christmas, Wayne," Lorna yelled accusingly.

"That's what got us into this mess," Wayne snarled. He turned to Packy. "All right, all right, I'll tell you. But only if you give me one more diamond—the one that looks like a robin's egg. You still have plenty more."

"If you have a lot of diamonds, I'd like one, too," Lorna said. "It could be a small one."

"There are no small ones," Packy snapped. "Covel, you want the robin's egg, and your lady friend wants a little one. You two ought to stick together. You're a real team. *Where's the flask?*"

"Have we got a deal?" Wayne asked. "I get the two diamonds. Don't worry about her."

"*The flask?*"

"But you still haven't promised."

"*I promise! I cross my heart and hope to die!*"

Wayne hesitated, shut his eyes, and opened them slowly. "I'm going to trust you. The flask is in the bottom drawer of the stove, inside a big pot with a missing handle."

In an instant Jo-Jo was on his knees, yanking open the drawer and tossing out pots, pans, and a rusty cookie sheet. The big pot was wedged in the drawer. Jo-Jo yanked at it so hard that the whole drawer came clattering out, sending him back on his heels. The big pot remained clutched in his hands. He opened it, looked inside, and reached in.

"This is it, huh, Packy?" He held up the flask.

Packy grabbed it from him, unscrewed the top, peeked inside, shook some of the diamonds into his hand, and cradled them lovingly as he sighed with relief. "Okay, it looks pretty full. Guess the one we found was the only one missing."

"The robin's egg?" Wayne reminded him.

"Oh, yeah, right." Carefully, Packy shook out more diamonds. "There it is—so big it can hardly get out. But that doesn't matter." He poured the diamonds back into the flask. Then he turned and his hand shot out. As he scooped the yellow diamond from Wayne's pocket, Wayne bit his finger.

"Ow!" Packy cried. "I'd better not get rabies."

"Wayne, I knew you shouldn't trust him!" Lorna cried. "You never get anything right."

An instant later Jo-Jo had taped their mouths.

Packy dangled the flask in front of Covel's eyes. "You think you're smart," he said. "Your girlfriend thinks she's smart. Too bad I don't have time to sell you both the Brooklyn Bridge. Anyone who believes a crook keeps his word shouldn't take up room in this world."

He and Jo-Jo started for the back door.

39

The Grangers turned down the dirt road marked "Dead End" and were forced to drive carefully because of the snow-covered ruts and crevices they were encountering. Behind them, Alvirah, Willy, Regan, and Jack agonized at the need to slow down. But then the Grangers stopped in front of a farmhouse, and their back door flew open.

"There it is!" Bobby cried, pointing.

"Get back in the car!" his mother ordered.

Jack pulled the Meehans' car onto the field in front of the house and stopped.

"This place looks deserted," Willy said as he looked from the house to the big barn.

They walked rapidly toward the house. "Look," Jack said, pointing to the side of the barn. "There's a white van with a ski rack."

Alvirah and Regan rushed to the porch and began peering in the windows. Alvirah grabbed Regan's arm. "There are cross-country skis on the floor there."

"Alvirah, they could be anybody's," Regan said.

"They're not anybody's," Alvirah said emphatically. "That's Opal's hat on the floor next to them! We've got to go in!"

"You're right, Alvirah," Willy agreed. He tried the front door and found it was locked. He picked up a chair on the porch and tossed it through the window. At their surprised reaction he said, "If we're wrong, I'll pay for the window, but I trust Alvirah's instincts."

The overpowering smell of gas hit them.

"Oh, my God," Alvirah cried. "If Opal's in there somewhere . . ."

In a moment Jack kicked out the rest of the glass, climbed in, and opened the door. His eyes were already watering from the effect of the gas.

"Opal!" Alvirah started screaming.

They ran through the downstairs floor, but there was no sign of anyone. In the kitchen Willy hurried to the stove and turned off a burner. "This is where the gas is coming from!"

Regan and Jack raced upstairs, Alvirah behind them. There were three bedrooms. The doors of all of them were closed.

"The gas isn't as strong up here," Regan said, coughing.

The first bedroom was empty. In the second one they could see a man tied to the bed. Alvirah threw open the third bedroom door and gasped. Opal was lying motionless, also tied to the bed.

"Oh, no!" Alvirah whispered. She ran to the bed, leaned down, and saw that Opal's lips were moving and her eyes were fluttering. "She's alive!"

Jack was next to her, quickly cutting the ropes with his pocket knife. Regan was putting one arm under Opal and lifting her up.

"If the bedroom doors hadn't been closed, these two would be dead by now," Jack said grimly. "Can you two handle Opal?"

"You bet we can," Alvirah said.

As Jack hurried into the other room, Regan and Alvirah draped Opal's arms over their shoulders and rushed her down the hall.

Jack and Willy were behind them, carrying a totally co-matose long-haired man.

Within seconds they were out the front door, off the porch, and hurrying to get a safe distance from the house.

"If we had rung that bell, we might have blown the whole place up," Jack said. "The way that downstairs was filled with gas, the electric discharge could have set off an explosion."

As they crossed the field, they heard a vehicle approaching. A pickup truck was barreling onto the property. Before the thought could even occur to them that it might be Opal's abductors returning, they saw Lem Pickens at the wheel. Without appearing to notice them, he whizzed past and came to a screeching halt next to the barn. As they watched, he raced to the doors, flung them open, and began to jump up and down.

"Our tree!" he yelled. "Our tree! I found our tree!" He rushed inside the barn to examine it.

"Their tree is here!" Regan exclaimed.

Opal was still draped over her and Alvirah's shoulders.

"Packy," Opal mumbled. "Diamonds. My money."

"Do you know where Packy is?" Alvirah asked her.

Lem came running out of the barn and raced over to them. "Our tree's fine. Just one branch broken!" He finally noticed what was going on in front of him. "What's the matter with these two?" he asked.

"They must have been drugged," Alvirah said. "And Packy Noonan is behind this."

"And so is this so-called poet," Lem declared, pointing at the sleeping Milo, still being supported by Willy and Jack.

"Wayne . . . has . . . diamonds. . . . Packy went there," Opal was mumbling.

"Where?" Regan asked her.

"Wayne's house. . . ."

"I knew Wayne Covel was in on this up to his ears!" Lem cried gleefully.

Regan turned to him. "Lem, you know the way to Wayne Covel's house. Ride with us there. Please! We can't waste a minute!"

Jack was on his cell phone, alerting the local police.

Lem looked back at the barn. "No way!" he shouted. "I can't let our tree out of my sight!"

Bobby Granger had escaped from his parents and came running toward them. "I'll mind your tree, mister," he called. "I won't let anybody touch it!"

"The police are on their way here and to Covel's house. Your tree will be fine," Jack said crisply. "Mr. Pickens, we really need your help. You know your way around this town."

The Grangers had caught up with their son. "We'll guard your tree," Bill Granger assured Lem.

"Well, all right," Lem said. "But tell them I have the keys to the flatbed in my pocket. I'm the one who'll drive it home to Viddy. But I'm not getting in any car with that poet."

"We'll mind him, too," Bill Granger said.

Alvirah got into the backseat of the Meehans' car. Then Jack lifted Opal in. Willy followed, to prop her up. Regan, Jack, and Lem
jumped into the front seat. Jack turned on the
ignition and drove as fast as he dared off the
property and onto the bumpy dirt road.

"Turn left up here," Lem ordered. "I knew
Wayne Covel, Packy Noonan, and that
so-called poet were all tarred with the same
brush. If you're looking for stolen goods, I
wouldn't be surprised at all to find the loot in
Wayne Covel's house. Now turn right."

Milo's beat-up car was on the other side of
the road, heading in the opposite direction.

"There's the poet's car!" Lem cried. "But
we know he's not driving!"

As it passed them, Alvirah shrieked, "It's
Packy Noonan driving!"

Jack did a U-turn and was caught behind a
delivery truck. The road was too narrow and
winding for him to pass. "Come on!" he said.
"Come on!"

When they came to an intersection, Milo's
battered heap was no longer in sight.

"They went thataway!" Lem pointed to the left.

"How do you know?" Jack asked.

"Look! The bumper is in the middle of the road there. It finally fell off that heap."

Regan had dialed the local police. She told them rapidly that they had spotted Packy Noonan and described the car to them and the direction it was headed. Next to her, Opal was mumbling, "Get him. Please. . . . All my money."

"We will, Opal," Regan promised. "Too bad you're not wide awake for this."

Around a bend they caught up with Milo's car, which was chugging along. Smiling broadly, Jack followed the old jalopy, speeding up when necessary to prevent another car from getting in between. In the distance they could see a police car speeding toward them, its lights flashing. Jack stopped to allow the police car to make a U-turn and get right behind Packy. A moment later the sound of a policeman's voice on the bullhorn could be heard even through the closed windows.

"Pull over, Packy. Don't get in any more trouble than you're in already."

A second police car went past Jack, and two more were coming from the opposite direction. Inside Milo's heap, Packy picked up the flask and handed it to Jo-Jo. "Get rid of it!" he ordered.

Jo-Jo opened the window, lowered his hand, and tossed it. The flask of diamonds rolled down the embankment.

"All that work swindling those dopey investors down the drain," Packy lamented wryly as he watched the flask disappear. He stopped the car and turned off the ignition.

"Come out with your hands up" came the command over the bullhorn as policemen poured from several patrol cars.

Jack stopped the car, and they all jumped out, except for Opal who slumped down on the backseat. Regan ran to the side of the road and backtracked about one hundred feet. Then, sliding and slipping, she made her way down the embankment. In the snow a metal flask was resting beneath a large evergreen tree. Regan picked it up, shook it, and heard a faint rattle. Smiling, she opened the cap. "My God," she murmured as she caught the first glimpse of the contents. She poured a few of the diamonds into her hand. "These have to be worth a fortune," she said to herself. "Wait till Opal sees this."

With infinite care she dropped the diamonds back into the flask and climbed up the embankment. She ran up to Packy Noonan who was now in handcuffs. "Is this the flask in your dreams, Packy?" she asked sarcastically. "The people who lost all their money in your shipping company are going to be mighty happy to see it."

A banging from the trunk of Milo's car startled them all. Guns drawn, two policemen threw the catch and stood back as the trunk swung up. Benny sat up, Jo-Jo's note still pinned to his jacket, and took in the whole scene. "I knew we shouldn't have gotten greedy," he said yawning. "Wake me up when we get to the police station." He lay back down and closed his eyes.

Regan turned to Alvirah. "Before we have to turn these over, let's show them to Opal."

They hurried back to their car, propped Opal into a sitting position, and wrapped her hands around the flask. "Opal, honey, look," Alvirah urged. "Stay awake long enough to look."

Regan unscrewed the cap.

"What?" Opal asked drowsily.

"These diamonds represent your lottery money. Now you'll get at least some of it back," Alvirah told her.

Drowsy as Opal was, the meaning of Alvirah's words penetrated her drugged brain, and she began to cry.

An hour later Lem Pickens was driving the flatbed through town, honking the horn incessantly. Beside him, Bobby Granger was waving to the cheering crowd that had gathered along the way. Finally, they were heading up the hill to Lem's home.

Alvirah, Willy, Regan, Jack, the Grangers, and a now more alert Opal were standing with

Viddy on the Pickenses' front porch. The word of the recovered tree had spread like wildfire. Media crews had hastily set up in the front yard to capture the moment when, still honking the horn, Lem Pickens triumphantly drove the Rockefeller Center flatbed onto his property. The look on Viddy's face when she saw her beloved blue spruce reminded Alvirah of the dazed joy she had seen on Opal's face, and like Opal, Viddy began to cry.

Epilogue

By the time the day of the Christmas tree lighting arrived, Lem and Viddy were practically seasoned New Yorkers. Two days after Lem recovered their tree, they were in Rockefeller Center watching its ceremonious arrival and listening to the choir of schoolchildren sing a medley of songs as the tree was raised into place. The selections from *The Sound of Music* especially delighted Viddy.

Edelweiss, she thought. Our blue spruce is my edelweiss.

They had been invited back for the party that Opal's fellow investors in the Patrick Noonan Shipping and Handling Company had thrown for her. The diamonds were valued at over seventy million dollars, so the investors would all recover at least two-thirds of their lost money.

Packy Noonan, Jo-Jo, and Benny were in prison awaiting trial and wouldn't set foot on a beach in Brazil or anywhere else for a long, long time. Milo had escaped with a slap on the wrist because of all the incriminating evidence he promised to offer and Opal's strong testimony that he had clearly been an unwilling participant who became entangled in a criminal web of deceit. Milo was now back in Greenwich Village, writing poems about betrayal. The $50,000 bonus the police found at the farmhouse was counterfeit. But he'd already won an award for a poem he wrote about a flatbed.

When the police had found Wayne Covel and his girlfriend Lorna tied up, Wayne tried to pretend he had no idea why Packy Noonan had done that to him. His testimony was shot down by the combined stories of Opal, Milo, Packy, Jo-Jo, and Benny. But as Wayne Covel then put it, "If it weren't for me, Packy Noonan would be in Brazil now with all the investors' money." He pleaded guilty to destroying the branch of the tree and claimed that he was trying to figure out how to return the diamonds without admitting how he got them. That story raised a few eyebrows, but in his plea bargain he was sentenced to only twelve hours of community service. Some community service they'll get out of that one, Viddy thought. His ex-girlfriend was back in Burlington, once again computer dating and looking for a kind and sensitive man. Lots of luck, Viddy thought.

The hardest pill Packy had to swallow was that he didn't know blue spruces grew from the top. He needn't have cut down the tree. His flask was the same distance from the ground as it had been when he tied it there. If he had known that, he and the twins could have just gone around to the back of the tree, found Wayne standing on the ladder, forced him off it, and cut the branch that held the flask.

Now Lem and Viddy were in the reserved section waiting for the tree to be lighted. Alvirah,

Willy, Regan, Jack, Nora, Luke, Opal, Opal's friend Herman Hicks, who Alvirah had told her was a recent lottery winner, and the three Grangers were with them. They'd all be heading back to Herman's apartment after the ceremony. It was a beautiful cool night. Rockefeller Center was overflowing with people, and the streets surrounding it were all blocked off.

"Viddy, you and Lem did a great job on the *Today Show* this morning," Regan said. "You're both naturals."

"You think so, Regan? Did my hair look all right?"

"It better have looked all right, with what it cost!" Lem observed.

"I loved having my makeup done," Viddy admitted. "I told Lem I want to have it done again when we come back for your wedding."

"Lord, help me," Lem mumbled.

Opal and Bobby were sitting next to each other. He turned to her. "I'm really glad I was in that ski group with you," he said.

"I am, too," Opal said.

"'Cause otherwise I wouldn't be here."

Opal laughed. "I wouldn't be here or any-where else!"

Herman took her hand. "Please don't say that, Opal."

"This is so beautiful," Alvirah sighed as she admired the whole spectacle.

Willy nodded and smiled. "Something tells me we'll be stopping by every night for the next month."

"Alvirah, we never did get a look at your maple syrup tree," Nora reminded her.

"Honey, we missed a lot of the excitement," Luke drawled.

"I don't need any more of that kind of excite-ment!" Opal protestd. "And believe me, from now on my money stays in a piggy bank. No more Packy Noonans in my life—the creep."

Christmas carols were being sung. It was one minute to the moment.

It's magical, Regan thought. Jack put his arm around her. That's magical, too, she thought with a smile.

The crowd started the countdown. "Ten, nine, eight . . ."

Lem and Viddy held their breaths and entwined their hands. They watched as in a brilliant and breathtaking moment the tree they had loved for fifty years was suddenly ablaze with thousands of colored lights, and everyone in the gathered throng began to cheer.

Scribner Proudly Presents

SANTA CRUISE

By Mary Higgins Clark and
Carol Higgins Clark

Now available in hardcover from Scribner

Please turn the page for a preview of
Santa Cruise. . . .

I

Randolph Weed, self-styled commodore, stood on the deck of his pride and joy, the *Royal Mermaid*, an old ship he had bought and paid a fortune to refurbish and on which he intended to spend the rest of his life playing host to both friends and paying guests. Docked in the Port of Miami, the ship was being readied for its maiden voyage, the "Santa Cruise," a four-day trip in the Caribbean with one stop at Fishbowl Island.

Dudley Loomis, Weed's forty-year-old PR man, who would also serve as cruise director, joined Randolph on the deck. He took a deep breath of the refreshing breeze blowing off the Atlantic Ocean and sighed happily. "Commodore, I have e-mailed all the major news organizations once again to let them know about this unique and wonderful maiden voyage. I began the release, 'On December 26th Santa is turning in his sleigh, giving Rudolph and the other reindeer some time off, and taking a cruise. It's the Santa Cruise—Commodore Randolph Weed's gift to a select group of people who have in their own unique way made the world a better place this past year.'"

"I've always liked giving gifts," the Commodore said, a smile on his weathered but still handsome sixty-three-year-old face. "But people didn't always appreciate it. My three ex-wives never understood what a deep and caring man I am. For goodness' sake, I gave the last wife my Google stock before it went public."

"That was a terrible mistake," Dudley said solemnly, shaking his head. "A terrible mistake."

"I don't begrudge her the money. I've made and lost fortunes. Now I want to give back to people. As you know, this Santa Cruise was created to raise money for charity, and celebrate those who have given of themselves."

"It was my idea," Dudley reminded him.

"True. But the money to pay for this cruise is coming out of my pocket. I spent considerably more than I expected in order to make the *Royal Mermaid* the beautiful ship she has become. But she's worth every penny." He paused. "At least I hope she is."

Dudley Loomis held his tongue. Everyone had warned the Commodore that he'd be better off having a new ship built than dumping a fortune into this old tub, but I *do* admit it cleaned up rather well, Dudley told himself. He had been cruise director on mammoth vessels where he had to worry about several thousand guests, many of whom he found intensely irritating. He would now deal with only four hundred passengers, most of whom would probably be happy to sit on deck and read instead of having entertainment shoved down their throats twenty-four hours a day. Dudley had come up with the idea of the Santa Cruise when reserva-

tions for passage on the *Royal Mermaid* were almost nil. He was a PR man right down to the
rubber soles of his yachting shoes.

"We should have a free cruise the day after
Christmas to get the kinks out of the ship before any paying passengers, or reviewers, come
on board," he had told his boss. "You'll donate
passage to charities and do-gooders. It'll only
be a few days, and in the long run it will pay for
itself with the good publicity I'll get for you. By
the time our real maiden voyage rolls around
on January 20th, we'll be turning people away.
You wait and see."

The Commodore had needed a few min-
utes to think about it. "A totally *free* cruise?"

"Free!" Dudley had insisted. "Everything
for free!"

The Commodore had winced. "The bar,
too?"

"Everything! From soup to nuts!"

Eventually, the Commodore agreed. Now,
the special Santa Cruise would set sail in one
week, the day after Christmas, and return to
Miami four days later.

As the two men walked along the freshly scrubbed deck, they went over the final details. "I'm still hoping for one of the television stations to at least attend the pre-sailing cocktail party on the deck," Dudley said. "I've sent word to the ten Santa Clauses you are treating to get here early, so they can try on the lightweight Santa Claus outfits that you had made for them. They should be ready to mingle with everyone at our evening cocktail party. It turned out to be a blessing in disguise when I had that fender bender with that Santa Claus from Tallahassee last month. While we were exchanging insurance papers, he teared up and confided how exhausting it was to listen to children all day long, have pictures taken with them, and, worse yet, be sneezed on. By the time Christmas Day rolled around, he'd be exhausted and unemployed again. That's when the light went on in my head to include ten Santas among the guests . . ."

"You're always thinking," the Commodore agreed. "I just hope we get enough paying passengers in the next few months to keep this ship afloat."

"It'll all be fine, Commodore," Dudley said in his most cheery cruise-director voice.

"You said we hadn't heard from all the people who won this trip at charity auctions. What's the status on that?"

"Everyone is coming—we're just waiting to hear from one passenger. She was by far the highest bidder at a charity auction for this cruise. I sent her a letter by FedEx, and as an enticement offered her the remaining two staterooms so she could bring friends. She's a good person for us to have aboard. She won forty million dollars in a lottery, appears on television regularly, and is a contributing columnist to a large newspaper." He did not add that he had lost the name and address of this winner from his friend Cal Sweeney's auction and had just followed up on it. He almost fainted when he realized Alvirah Meehan was not only a celebrity, but a columnist.

"Splendid, Dudley, splendid. I wouldn't

mind winning the lottery myself! In fact, I may need to . . ."

"Good morning, Uncle Randolph."

They had not heard the Commodore's nephew, Eric, come up behind them.

Sneaky as always, Dudley thought as he turned to greet the newcomer. I swear he could make his living as a mugger.

"Good morning, my boy," the Commodore said heartily, beaming at his kinsman.

The warm smile on thirty-two-year-old Eric Manchester's face was the expression he reserved for the Commodore and other important people, Dudley observed. With his perfect tan, sun-streaked hair, and muscled body, Eric had obviously divided his time between the beach and the gym. He was wearing a Tommy Bahama floral shirt, khaki shorts, and docksiders. The sight of him made Dudley ill. He knew that when the passengers came on board Eric would be outfitted as an officer of the ship, although God knows what office he was supposed to hold.

How come I wasn't born good-looking, with a rich uncle, Dudley wondered wistfully.

"I'm running into town, sir," Eric addressed the Commodore, totally ignoring Dudley. "Anything you need?"

"I'll let you two chat," Dudley said, anxious to get away from the farce of watching Eric pretend he was of any use to the Commodore, the *Royal Mermaid*, or the upcoming Santa Cruise. Eric had wormed his way onto the payroll immediately after his uncle bought the ship.

The Commodore smiled at his sister's son. "Don't need a thing I don't already have," he said heartily. "Have fun at the party you went to last night?"

Eric thought of the wad of cash he'd been given at that party, the down payment on what would make the Santa Cruise a risky and dangerous trip—and profitable for him . . . "It was lots of fun, Uncle Randolph," Eric said. "I was bragging to everyone about our upcoming Santa Cruise and how generous you are helping to raise money for charities. Everyone there wished they were coming with us."

The Commodore slapped him on the back. "Good work, Eric. Get people interested in us. Get people to sign up for one of our voyages."

I did, Eric thought, but you won't know about them . . . He shivered slightly, yet he couldn't help but smile at the irony.

Eric's guests would be the only two paying passengers on the Santa Cruise.

2

At seven P.M. on December 23rd, a light snow was falling on New York City as last-minute shoppers and partygoers scurried through the streets of Manhattan. In the festively decorated Grill Room of the Four Seasons restaurant on Fifty-second Street, just off Park Avenue, lottery winners Alvirah and Willy Meehan and their good friends, suspense writer Nora Regan Reilly and her funeral-director husband, Luke, were all sipping glasses of wine. They were awaiting the arrival of Nora and Luke's only offspring, Regan, and her new husband, Jack, whose surname also happened to be Reilly.

The two couples had met exactly two years earlier, when Luke had been kidnapped by the disgruntled heir of one of his deceased clients. Alvirah had been a cleaning woman who had won forty million dollars in the lottery and then became an amateur sleuth. She had introduced herself to Regan and helped in the frantic search to save Luke. In the process, Regan had met Jack, who was head of the Major Case Squad in Manhattan, and they had fallen in love. As Luke observed, "It's an ill wind that blows no one good."

Now, Alvirah, her ample figure smartly dressed in a dark blue cocktail suit, was bursting with the invitation she intended to extend to the four Reillys, but also trying to figure out how to make it an invitation they couldn't refuse.

Willy, her husband of forty-three years who, with his white hair, map-of-Ireland face, and generous girth, was the living image of the late, legendary Speaker of the House Tip O'Neill, had been no help to her on the cab ride over from their apartment on Central Park South.

"Honey," he'd said. "All you can do is invite them. They'll say 'yes' or they'll say 'no.'"

Now Alvirah looked across the table at petite Nora, elegant as always in a deceptively simple black dress, and six-foot-five Luke, towering beside her, his arm loosely around the back of her chair. We always have fun and excitement when we go on trips together, she thought, then realized that her idea of fun might be their idea of too much excitement.

"Oh, here they are," Nora exclaimed as Regan and Jack came up the stairs, spotted them, waved, and started over to the table.

Alvirah sighed with joy. She absolutely loved this young couple. Regan had her mother's blue eyes and fair skin, but she was four inches taller than Nora and had inherited her black hair from her father's side of the family. Jack, six feet two with sandy hair, hazel eyes, and a firm jaw, had an air of no-nonsense self-confidence that had made her sure from the get-go that he was the right man for Regan.

Jack apologized for keeping them waiting. "A few last-minute things came up at the office, but it could have been worse. I'm happy to report that as of now and for the next two weeks, Regan Reilly Reilly and I are at liberty."

It was the opening Alvirah needed. She waited until the captain poured wine for the newcomers, then raised her own glass in a toast. "To sharing a wonderful holiday season," she said. "I have a terrific surprise for the four of you, but first you'll have to promise you'll say 'yes.'"

Luke looked alarmed. "Alvirah, knowing you, I can't make a promise like that without knowing a lot more details."

"I wouldn't either," Willy agreed. "This is what it's about. We got roped into attending a charity auction. Need I explain more? You've been to plenty of them yourselves. Once they started the live auction after dinner, I knew we were in for trouble. Alvirah got that look on her face . . ."

"Willy, it was for a good cause," Alvirah protested.

"They're all good causes. Ever since we won the lottery, we've been on the list for every good cause known to man."

"It's true," Alvirah admitted with a laugh. "But I went to this one because it was being chaired by Mrs. Sweeney's son, Cal. She's the lady I used to clean for on Tuesdays. Cal is a trustee of their local hospital, and it needs help. Anyhow I got carried away, I admit, and I won a Caribbean cruise for two. I never heard another word about it and didn't realize it was a Christmas cruise. It's been such a crazy year that I forgot all about it until this afternoon, to be honest, when a FedEx envelope arrived from a cruise director. There had been some kind of slipup, and the cruise I won at the auction is set for next week. It leaves on December 26th and comes back on the 30th."

"Three days from now! That's mighty short notice," Jack said. "Are you going to go? If not, you could probably force them to put you on a different cruise. It's their fault you didn't get sufficient notice."

"But this is a very special voyage," Alvirah explained eagerly. "They're calling it the Santa Cruise. Everyone on board is someone who either won the trip by being the highest bidder in a charity auction; or who is a part of a group that did a great deal of good helping other people during the year; or who, after submitting proof of making a generous donation to a worthwhile charity, was selected in a random lottery."

"You mean no one's *paying?*" Luke asked incredulously as he accepted a menu from the waiter. "That cruise line must be rolling in cash!"

"I have the brochure with lots of pictures and all the details," Alvirah said, reaching down and fishing it out of her purse. "The ship looks gorgeous. It's brand new. Well *almost* brand new—it was refurbished from stem to stern. If you can believe it, it even has a helicopter pad and a rock climbing wall, just like all the new big ships. The best part is that the cruise director is so apologetic about the notification mix-up that he wants us to bring four people as our guests to make up for it, and he offered two luxury rooms with balconies—just like our cabin.

She beamed at the four Reillys. "I want you all to sail on the Santa Cruise with us."

"Oh, that's impossible," Nora answered quickly, shaking her head and looking at Luke to back her up.

"Aaaah, we're just planning to relax next week . . ." Luke began, clearing his throat as he tried to think of a stronger excuse.

"How better to relax than on a cruise?" Alvirah insisted. "Think about it. You two are going to the South of France after the first of the year. Regan, I know you and Jack are meeting friends in Lake Tahoe on New Year's Eve. What do you have planned for those four days after Christmas that beats sailing in the Caribbean?"

It was a rhetorical question. "Regan," Alvirah continued, "I just heard from Jack's own lips that he's on vacation for two weeks. What are you committed to do the day after Christmas and the three days after that?"

"Absolutely nothing," Regan said promptly. "Jack, we've never been on a cruise together. I think it would be fun."

"The weather prediction for the New York area next week is freezing to frigid or the other way around, whichever is colder," Willy said encouragingly. He knew that in the couple of hours since that FedEx package arrived Alvirah had set her heart on having the Reillys join them on the cruise. "We're hiring a private plane to fly us to Miami on the 26th," he added, hoping that Alvirah wouldn't admit that this was the first she'd heard of *that* plan. "Think about it. A beautiful ship. Fine people as our fellow passengers. Swimming in the outdoor pool in December. Sitting on the deck reading a book. I'll bet lots of the people will be reading your books, Nora. What do you say?"

"It sounds too good to be true," Nora said matter-of-factly, but then she paused a moment and added, "I certainly know that we always have a great time with you guys, and I definitely would enjoy spending quality time with my child and brand-new son-in-law."

Alvirah smiled triumphantly. She could tell that the Reillys were going to go on the cruise with them. Nora and Regan were getting excited about it already and Luke and Jack would fall in line, however reluctantly. As they toasted to sharing the Santa Cruise, Alvirah was glad she'd never brought up the fact that yesterday, at yet another charity luncheon, she'd had a reading by a psychic who had been hired as a gimmick to raise extra money. As soon as her cards were dealt, the psychic's eyes had widened to the point that her eyelids had disappeared into her skull. "*I see a tub,*" she had whispered. "*A large tub. You are not safe in it. Listen to me. Your body must not be surrounded by water. Until after the new year you must only take showers.*"